DEADMAN'S FLOAT

"Mr. Barefoot? Is that you?"

Winston listened. Silence. No sound came from the boathouse on his left. A few feet to his right, the path led to a stone outcropping that held two picnic tables.

A piece of floating debris caught Winston's attention. It has risen in the water, shone white in the sunlight, then sank. Winston took two steps and stopped. One of those plastic gloves, he assured himself.

Out on the Hudson, a pleasure craft passed, sending toward shore a rolling wave of water. Reaching the land, the wave did a diver's turn and, coming up ten feet out in the river as a burst of white spray, brought with it Justin Barefoot. There was no mistaking the long nose and the haughty mouth formed into a perfect "O" of surprise.

As he watched, the body slowly turned over. Justin Barefoot was out there, face down in the Hudson, and he wasn't doing the crawl.

THE BEST IN CONTEMPORARY SUSPENSE

WHERE'S MOMMY NOW? (366, $4.50)
by Rochelle Majer Krich

Kate Bauers couldn't be a Superwoman any more. Her job, her demanding husband, and her two children were too much to manage on her own. Kate did what she swore she'd never do: let a stranger into her home to care for her children. *Enter Janine.*

Suddenly Kate's world began to fall apart. Her energy and health were slipping away, and the pills her husband gave her and the cocoa Janine gave her made her feel worse. Kate was so sleepy she couldn't concentrate on the little things—like a missing photo, a pair of broken glasses, a nightgown that smelled of a perfume she never wore. Nobody could blame Janine. Everyone loved her. Who could suspect a loving, generous, jewel of a mother's helper?

COME NIGHTFALL (340, $3.95)
by Gary Amo

Kathryn liked her life as a successful prosecuting attorney. She was a perfect professional and never got personally involved with her cases. Until now. As she viewed the bloody devastation at a rape victim's home, Kathryn swore to the victim to put the rapist behind bars. But she faced an agonizing decision: insist her client testify or to allow her to forget the shattering nightmare.

Soon it was too late for decisions: one of the killers was out on bail, and he knew where Kathryn lived. . . .

FAMILY REUNION (375, $3.95)
by Nicholas Sarazen

Investigative reporter Stephanie Kenyon loved her job, her apartment, her career. Then she met a homeless drifter with a story to tell. Suddenly, Stephanie knew more than she should, but she was determined to get this story on the front page. She ignored her editor's misgivings, her lover's concerns, even her own sense of danger, and began to piece together a hideous crime that had been committed twenty years ago.

Then the chilling phone calls began. And the threatening letters were delivered. And the box of red roses . . . dyed black. Stephanie began to fear that she would not live to see her story in print.

A WINSTON WYC MYSTERY
THE DUTCH TREAT MURDERS
BRIAN JOHNSTON

PINNACLE BOOKS
WINDSOR PUBLISHING CORP.

For Colin.
Special thanks to Christopher Gray.

PINNACLE BOOKS

are published by

Windsor Publishing Corp.
475 Park Avenue South
New York, NY 10016

First printing: December, 1991

Printed in the United States of America

Chapter 1

Verplanck Dace, known as Dutch to his few friends, lowered the body gently into the dark water, like a mother offering her baby its first bath. The important difference was that this body didn't need a wash. It was dead. Dutch gave the inert bundle one more going over. The knots seemed okay and the anchor should keep it down until it didn't matter. Rolly had insisted on tying a cloth over the man's eyes. Said he couldn't stand the idea of fish eating them out. Stretching to his right, Dutch twisted the body down and toward him, allowing water entry into the pant legs. Air trapped in the trousers had billowed them up to mid thigh where the rope was pulled tight. No need for a man to look foolish at his moment of parting.

"You got anything to say?"

Dutch spoke softly. Voices carried great distances over water and it was a calm night.

"Only I hope he's happy."

Rolly wasn't completely happy himself, noted Dutch. Dead people weren't part of the plan. It added a serious note to the whole affair.

"What's that supposed to mean?"

5

"I'm not sure."

Dutch gave Rolly one of his looks.

"You know, like he's finally found the peace he couldn't have here on earth. That sort of thing."

Dutch nodded and gave the man a pat on the head.

"God rest your soul, pal. You came a long way for nothing."

The two men watched until the last of the vertical line of bubbles broke the surface of the water. Dutch moved quietly to the bridge. Morning would break over Trap Rock soon. The twin MAN 680 horsepower diesel engines had been idling for so long their rumble had become part of the background noise. Now, as he eased open the throttle, the rumble coughed into a roll of thunder beneath them and Dutch hoped he sounded like a shad fisherman out early. Reaching down, he flicked on the running lights. It had been warm that night and the fog hadn't developed as he wished it might, but luck was still on his side and they'd made no contact the entire trip. Too bad it had ended so . . . differently. There'd be some explaining. Stretching his neck, Dutch sucked the wind in through his mouth, letting the wet spray coat his dry throat.

Verplanck Dace was a "long drink of water" as Rolly would say. Tall and sinewy, the seventy-five year old man still didn't look old enough for retirement. People always marveled that he should be over sixty. He thought them silly. The secret was there for them too if they cared, but they'd never believe him, or worse, think him a fool. It was the Hudson. The river kept him young. He had learned early how to open up to it, how to listen, how to accept the river into his being. He used its revitalizing energy, its power to flush out his tension and pain. Wasn't it stress that turned people old? Gave them the lines,

6

the bad stomach, the need. It was river water that circulated in Dutch Dace's veins and all that went with it—the shad, the herring, the madtom, the kokanee, the red silt brought down from Lake Tear of the Clouds and the ocean that rushed in and out each day to meet it. He looked down into the black water. Of course chance also had its say in how long things lasted. Rolly moved beside him.

"What you going to tell Mom, Dutch?"

"Tell her what happened. The truth. Nothing else for it."

"Yeah, I guess so."

Dutch could see this might have been Rolly's last trip North. Up ahead the light of the boathouse could be seen.

"I'd like to be settled into the sea when I go," said Dutch into the blackness. Carried around the world by the secret currents. Visit *Hyorky* as the real old-timers called it, that place where you want to be but can never seem to find, no matter how far you travel. Those men who remembered the whaling ships that came far up the river to the friendlier ports of New Holland and Hudson. Ships that hired on the farm boys to carry them away to strange places—strange adventures.

"Sea? This is a river, Dutch. The Hudson, remember?" Rolly shook his head and stared over to the boathouse. "You sure talk funny sometimes. Mom says it's from living your whole life alone."

I ain't alone, thought Dutch. Never have been, never will be. It would be hard to explain to most people. Reducing the engines, he eased the fifty foot motor craft toward its mooring. Sunlight hit the dock the same time he did.

Chapter 2

Winston Wyc nearly missed the small porcelain plaque mounted on the gate post. Having followed the twelve foot high brick wall for nearly half a mile, he had become intrigued by its size and length, particularly the crushed glass set in cement at the top. A delicate touch to keep the light-fingered at bay. Or was it the common folk? The robber baron who had built this wall might have laughed at the growing security industry of today, all too ready to convince him of the need for expensive electronic sensors and monitoring screens. Pointed shards of glass were cheap and visibly discouraging.

Mr. Conran had said to go straight through Buddingville and "follow the brick wall for a short way" until he came to the gate. Winston hadn't expected the Great Wall of China that continued beyond the gate, disappearing around the bend up ahead. A short way in the city was five flights down to the street by stairs and directly into the Korean produce market next door. All other distances had to be negotiated. Eager to enter behind this brick barrier, he checked his rear view mirror and brought the rented Mercury to a stop. Backing up, Winston eased over until he was abreast of the gate.

Oblates of Tranquil Deliverance, read the neatly printed sign. The word Private, bolder and more visible underneath.

Deliverance should always be private and most certainly tranquil, thought Winston. Having just driven up from New York City, the idea had its appeal.

Slipping the Mercury past the opened wrought iron gates, Winston paused at a fieldstone guardhouse. No one seemed in attendance and Winston, taking this as a sign of welcome, left behind the world of highways and speed and entered onto the quiet, manicured grounds of what might have been an English manor estate. Trees, separated by wide expanses of clipped lawn, had grown to immense and majestic sizes. Here and there a park bench waited in a tree's shade. In the distance, a yew hedge hid what might be a garden labyrinth. Nature seemed suddenly to relax; her grass greener, her foliage fuller, her birds happier. The wall successfully erased the sights and sounds of the hustle beyond its height. Winston entertained the possibility of leaving his car at the side of the drive and walking the remaining distance to the castle, but his better judgment interceded. The castle was not yet visible and might be another mile or so. The city brain had no defenses against the seductive, decent properties of country air. If Winston weren't careful, he'd soon be exercising in the grass.

The road wandered through the grounds like a tired stream, following the natural contours of the land, giving in to any obstacle. Its many twists and turns kept the driving slow and the eye focused on the ingenuity of the gardener's art. One idyllic scenario after another presented itself for praise: a fieldstone retaining wall covered in yellow sedum; slender, ionic columns supporting an arbor of wild roses; an embankment of lavender Veronica highlighted by sharp, white blossoms of phlox, all cascading down into a pool of water. Winston felt the trials of driving two hours ebb from his body. By the time he reached the house he would not only be delivered but surely tranquil. And why not? Inquiries had informed him that his latest client was one of the most expensive weekend retreats in the Hudson Valley, specializing in burned-out yuppies and overwrought, underfed society ladies positively "unable to endure" another weekend of dealing with caterers and grumpy husbands. Following this afternoon's consultation, Winston was planning to head back to the city, taking a much needed week's vacation. Tonight he would fall asleep nestled in the arms of the Sherry-Netherland. The grounds of this monastic retreat appeared to be the perfect place to begin a restful week.

While waiting for two geese to cross the road, Winston refreshed his memory concerning the estate's history. The Oblates had bought the old Smelton estate, a thousand acres along the Hudson River, ten years ago from the last of the Smeltons. Thomas Smelton the Umpteenth had fried his brain early in life, preferring alcohol and drugs to industry. No one was quite sure where he had disappeared with the enormous check he'd received. The first Thomas Smelton had become extremely wealthy buying up surplus army goods cheap and selling it for mucho pesos to various revolutionaries in South America. In 1902 he purchased the land along the Hudson River and built his retirement home, a thirty bedroom Scottish castle that had been brought, stone by stone, from the old country. Here he lived in baronial splendor until his death in 1920 when, on a bet, he was lost trying to swim across the river. The family watched with varying degrees of feigned horror from their picnic blankets as Squire Thomas sank forever beneath the waters. Mrs. Smelton moved back to the Fifth Avenue house, never again to see her magnificent, much loved gardens. The estate passed from one Smelton to another until Thomas the Umpteenth sold it to the Oblates of Tranquil Deliverance.

Mr. Conran, the director of the retreat, had called Winston a month ago asking him to represent the retreat's governing board in its quest for entry onto the National Register of Historic Places in Washington. Mr. Wyc had been highly recommended by the New Holland Historical Society. Which wasn't all that flattering, thought Winston. Being one of the few architectural historians outside the academic community, Winston found himself more and more acting as a consultant and chief paper shuffler to a growing number of people and organizations that wished to preserve their small piece of the historic pie. Only a few years ago the state or local historic society had been happy to send someone to your home at no cost to assist you in filling out the necessary forms and getting you on your way. But as so often happens, as interest and applications dramatically increased, the feds cut government funding and made the process five times as complicated, even eliminating the free service. Now you had to have the help of a specially trained consultant and this is where Winston was finding most of his work. This was okay with him; even if the process was a little on the tedious side, it paid the rent. Architectural historians didn't actually laugh when they went to the bank.

At first Winston had been hesitant about accepting the Oblates' job, for he didn't like leaving the safety of New York City. Odd things tended to happen when Winston crossed over into rural areas, but the chance to see Smelton Castle and explore its parapets had won him over. An architectural historian can be easily beguiled when a castle is the enticement.

The landscape fell away suddenly in a long cascade of lawn that ended at the banks of the Hudson River, a quarter of a mile below. The road dipped and curved to the left and Winston found himself staring up at a forty foot high, masonry wall supported by two large, towers. Balconied windows looked down from what must have been the third floor. The wall was capped with the crenelated battlements of a medieval fortress. The drive curved to the right and Winston could see a portion of the front. A two hundred and fifty foot long curtain wall joined another tower at the far end. In the midsection of the expanse two small towers flanked a door wide enough to admit a car. Rising behind this wall was a structure six stories high topped with a mansard roof, many fanciful chimney pots, and what looked to Winston to be two highly ornamented belvederes, all contained by a perpendicular parapet. Turrets with lancet windows and coned roofs were corbeled out from every corner. Winston half expected Tinkerbell to fly out from one of the oriel windows that protruded from the face of the structure and sprinkle him with magic dust. The picture that Mr. Conran had sent to Winston had been taken from the opposite bank of the Hudson River and against the majestic vistas of the river the structure had appeared, if somewhat fanciful, harmonious and well-intentioned like those postcards one sees of castles in Europe taken from the air. Amazing how one hundred rooms doesn't seem all that imposing from a mile away. Hardly affects the landscape at all. Somewhere back on the thruway, Winston had magically made a wrong turn and here he was, twenty miles outside London, about to share tea and small talk with Prince Charles. And how *is* Di, Chuck? Another scone? Why, thank you.

Signs printed in a Gallic style and reading Reception directed Winston around the near tower, along the wall, and up to the large, arched opening. The entrance was blocked by a massive wooden grating. Winston wondered if he was supposed to get out and ring a bell, pull a chain or signal his arrival by blowing on a trumpet. Noticing a small door set into the grid of this barrier, Winston was about to get out and knock when the whole structure, with a great rattling of chains and scraping of metal, began moving upward. Holding his breath, Winston waited for it to stop making noise before he drove quickly through the passageway and into a large, cobbled parking area. The tall structure Winston had spied from the outside rose directly opposite the entrance, overshadowing the inner courtyard. Two identical, smaller buildings flanked the taller one and were built up against the curtain walls that defined the sides of the castle. Winston was impressed. That old federal income tax had sure put a damper on how the wealthy spent their fortunes nowadays.

Winston watched as a woman bounded through the front door of the main building and hurried across the cobbles to where he sat parked. There was a self-confidence about the woman that underscored her agitated approach. Her soft, blond hair was neither too long nor too short; her dark, tailored suit was all business but not at all aggressive. Her low heels handled the cobblestones easily. Winston climbed from the car to meet her.

"Mr. Wyc?"

"Yes . . ."

"Mr. Wyc, you've snuck up on us."

"I have?"

The woman paused to catch her breath. A deep inhale and then a hard, contained exhale. This followed by a sudden, sensible smile and a hand shake. All under control now.

"I'm Cynthia Shea. We didn't expect you until around one and the man at the guardhouse was to give us a call upon your arrival. Did you see him?"

Winston shook his head. Cynthia Shea was in her early thirties and attractive in a scrubbed, aerobically tight way. That is, all the parts looked gym-toned and under control. No inch to pinch here. It always bothered Winston that people so slender could exert such robustness.

"I wonder where he is. Oh well, you're here." Cynthia looked toward the house and then back to Winston. Taking him into her confidence, she lowered her voice slightly. "Mr. Conran and I wanted to speak to you before you met the rest of the board. Two of the members . . ." She paused, thinking about those troublesome two and shook her head. ". . . seem to have taken offense at this whole historic designation thing. Shall we walk?" Cynthia began to lead Winston away from the main door and over to one of the side buildings.

"We, Mr. Conran and I, had thought the idea was unanimous but . . ."

"Cynthia!"

"Damn," Cynthia muttered under her breath. Winston turned to watch a tall, aristocratic looking gentleman descend the front steps, his arm raised above his head as if hailing a taxi. Following close

14

behind came a shorter man who had also raised his arm in imitation but without the authority of the first man. Winston noted the second man appeared afraid of the cobblestones, keeping his head down and picking his way across the courtyard as if fording a stream. The first man came to a stop with a huff.

"Cynthia, is this the fellow?"

The man eyed Winston as he might have some counterfeit art work. Cynthia narrowed her eyes and in a clipped manner made the introductions.

"Justin, this is Mr. Wyc, the architectural historian. Mr. Wyc, Mr. Justin Barefoot."

Mr. Barefoot made no move to present his hand. Behind him, the second man gave a small cough.

"And Mr. Eric Shrove," continued Cynthia, "Mr. Wyc."

"I'm pleased to meet you. My father was interested in history, you know. In fact, many nights were spent . . ."

"Mr. Wyc, if it wasn't for the decency of *some* people we would not have been aware of your visit." Mr. Barefoot cut Mr. Shrove short by giving him a curt glare of impatience. Winston thought he detected a trace of a Southern accent in Mr. Barefoot's voice.

"You didn't get one of my flyers?" said Winston.

"What?" Mr. Barefoot drew back slightly.

"He's kidding, Justin." Cynthia gave Winston her are-you-all-there look. She turned back to Mr. Barefoot. "And, why are you blowing this all out of proportion?"

"Am I? If Melody hadn't called me about this little meeting here, I would have known nothing about it. You and Conran and . . . this fellow would have convinced her to go the way of land conserving or whatever it's called and left me and Eric none the wiser."

15

"That's right," said Eric.

"Who said I was all for the idea?" asked Cynthia.

"If I may explain myself . . ." Winston raised a finger for emphasis.

"What's to explain? Do you know what this land is worth, Mr. Wyc? Do you have any idea?"

"Mr. Wyc doesn't care how much the land is worth, Justin. He is a stranger in a strange land, here to give us information. Nothing more, nothing less."

Winston had been watching the man approach. It was difficult not to. A huge man dressed in a baby blue cowl, he appeared to be the largest ecclesiastical robin's egg ever laid. Coming up from behind Cynthia Shea, he stuck out his hand.

"Mr. Wyc, I'm Michael Conran. We've talked on the phone."

Brushing back his hood with a quick flip of his hand, Mr. Conran presented Winston with a magnanimous smile, every magnificent crinkle and dimple shouting welcome. The cropped, white hair—a tight halo keeping the radiant countenance from spilling out into the parking lot. The intelligent, gray eyes contradicted the cheerfulness to some degree but not enough to interfere. If the man wanted to ham it up a little, he nevertheless played his part well.

"Hello. There seems to be some problem with my presence," Winston remarked.

"Problem?" boomed Mr. Conran. "Nonsense. Merely a misunderstanding, an overreaction maybe but not a problem. Mr. Barefoot is upset because I had not contacted him about your coming. I didn't think it all that important he should be here, which for him is a considerable trip."

"Me too," interjected the cautious voice of Eric Shrove.

"Hogwash," said Mr. Barefoot. "I'm not one to overreact and Virginia's not that far in this day and age. You wanted to corrupt Melody Pinklingill with your talk of historical preservation and not have me here to balance the scales."

"Who's Melody Pinklingill?" asked Winston.

"She's the fifth board member," answered Cynthia. "The rest of us here comprise the entire board. She lives here in Buddingville."

"She's sort of old," offered Eric Shrove.

"Miss Pinklingill may be along in years ..." added Mr. Conran. ". . . but she's certainly in possession of all her mental faculties. Melody is quite capable of making her own decisions."

"Hogwash. She's been around the corner for five years now. Ever since her accident." Mr. Barefoot went to poke Mr. Conran in the chest with his finger but thought better of it. "Everybody knows it."

"Could I make a suggestion?" Winston raised his voice slightly. They all turned to peer at him as if he'd burped. "What I have to say will only take half an hour. Why don't we go inside, let me deliver my spiel and then, while I'm showing myself around the castle, the board can discuss the merits, good or otherwise, of preservation."

Winston tried out a warm smile.

"Of course Mr. Wyc is right," said Mr. Conran. "We're acting foolish. Let me say this now for all those present: I am glad everyone's here. Nothing will get misconstrued in the repeating. Mr. Wyc can enlighten us about the preservation process. . . ." He raised his hand to silence Mr. Barefoot. ". . . and then we'll all know what's involved. It does not mean we accept the process. Let's think of it as a learning experience. Then maybe a little lunch and a tour for Mr. Wyc."

Without waiting for differences of opinion, Mr. Conran turned abruptly and headed back to the main building. Winston watched as the others hesitantly turned and walked single file behind him. Getting his briefcase from the car, Winston shook his head and prepared himself for an afternoon in rural fantasyland. Glancing up to see if the parapets were manned, he noticed what appeared to be a nun standing on a second floor balcony, cautioning a glance at him, but the image had stepped back quickly and he wasn't sure. Was the help attired in medieval garb? Part of the show? Lingering behind the others, Mr. Shrove waited at the door for him to approach.

"Quite the door, eh?" said Mr. Shrove proudly, his face an embarrassed pinch.

Winston stopped to inspect the curved top, oaken door. Four feet wide and three inches thick with an exposed cut nail driven in every two inches, it could have repelled the surliest of Huns. Large strap hinges shaped like dragons rounded out the fortress look. Centered in the door was a lion's head knocker that could have been used to open coconuts.

"Certainly in keeping with the general theme," offered Winston.

"Architectural historian sounds like fun, Mr. Wyc."

"Call me Winston, please. And it can be. Sometimes."

"Of course. Look, don't mind us. This group argues all the time. How we ever got together . . . oh well. This whole question of preservation has *me* confused. Although, don't get me wrong! I'm really very much for saving our national treasures."

"We should all be concerned. What do you do, Mr. Shrove?"

"Eric. Call me Eric." Pronouncing his first name

seemed to embarrass Mr. Shrove who put his head down and giggled. Winston was reminded of the Pillsbury doughboy.

"I have a small accounting business down in Washington. Much like H. and R. Block but regional. Very regional." Mr. Shrove said this rather wistfully. "We do well though, don't get me wrong."

Winston was sure he did. This sheepish, little man was probably hell on wheels in a pile of tax forms.

"How did you become involved with the Oblates of Tranquil Deliverance? It doesn't seem your cup of tea."

"Ohhhh . . . I did it as an investment you might say." Mr. Shrove giggled again. "Actually, if the truth be known, I'm really . . ."

"What are you doing, Eric?" Mr. Barefoot loomed out of the entryway. "Mr. Wyc has a presentation to deliver and a long drive back to New York City. Let's not keep him waiting."

"We can call him Winston, Justin."

"Can we?" Mr. Barefoot tried to look down his long nose at Winston, but since they were the same height he quickly gave up and opted instead for a puckered expression of disdain. "Well then, let's show . . . Winston . . . to the library." Justin waited for Eric to pass him. "Follow me, Winston."

Winston entered a small anteroom lined with oak benches and wooden pegs for hanging one's coat or armor. Through an archway he passed into a large, entrance hall off of which were many doors. At the far end, wide, stone stairs led up to a mezzanine that ran around three sides of the room. The mezzanine was supported by oak bracing that had been carved in the form of arms with the palms of the hands facing upward, the fingers lifted and spread to hold up the support timbers of the balcony. The entrance area acted as a reception room and was furnished with several Gothic Revival side chairs and a very uncomfortable looking Windsor settee. No need for the clientele to hang about the foyer. A long, refectory table along the left wall held a variety of brochures explaining the history of the castle and the expected deportment of those using the facilities. A young woman in a flowered blouse and spandex leggings stood to the left of the table. Her attractive but insincere face was framed in the latest teenage hair style, which is to say, her hair looked as if she were standing in front of a powerful fan aimed straight at the back of her head. Although barely out of her teens, she had already mastered that phony smile so well honed by aging receptionists and funeral home directors. Everyone else had moved on to another room except Justin Barefoot, who stood waiting and looking irritated over by a door on Winston's right.

"Welcome to Smelton Castle, Mr. Wyc," said the insincere smile. "I'm Ms. Yeats. I work in the office over there . . ." Ms. Yeats indicated a door to her right. ". . . and I'll be glad to provide you with any information or answer any questions you might have concerning the operation of the retreat. No one knows it better than I." She paused in her recital to give Winston an appraising once over.

"How did the front door know to open when I arrived?" asked Winston. "I didn't see anyone."

Ms. Yeats's eyes showed signs of life as she held a guffaw back with both her hands. "That's my secret," she said through her fingers.

"Your arrival is recorded by a camera," Mr. Barefoot announced from his doorway. "Ms. Yeats can see you on a monitor in her office, Mr. Wyc. She then presses a button. Now, shall we join the others in the library?"

Ms. Yeats's eyes became more hooded, her mouth forming a sullen circle of hate; a female Stanley Kowalski. If looks could maim, Mr. Barefoot would have been in deep trouble.

"Your secret's safe with me," said Winston.

Sucking in her cheeks, Ms. Yeats turned her hooded eyes in Winston's direction.

"Nice table," said Winston to no one in particular. "English. Around 1650 I'd say. That come with the castle?"

"Yes it did," Justin answered.

Winston's expertise in the furniture line seemed to surprise Mr. Barefoot.

"You know antiques, Mr. Wyc?"

"It's difficult to study architecture of the past and not pick up some knowledge of the furniture used. Often they went hand in hand."

"I understand that to be the case."

"Are you a collector, Mr. Barefoot?"

"Yes I am. It's my business."

Winston nodded to Ms. Yeats.

"If I need anything I'll come a calling. Thanks."

"Sure thing, Mr. Wyc."

Waiting for Winston to pass him before speaking, Mr. Barefoot forced a conversational tone as the two men walked down a long corridor.

"There's another entry on the river side of the castle, Mr. Wyc. Mr. Smelton used to bring his guests up the Hudson by steamer, putting them ashore down by the boat house. Horse drawn cabriolets would convey them to a portico attached rather creatively on the west side of the castle."

"People arrive by motor now, I take it. No more arrivals by water?"

"Oh, some come by way of water. The monastery has a boat for just that purpose. They consider the

21

trip up the river the beginning of the deliverance process. Much more soothing than traveling by highway."

And much more expensive, thought Winston, wondering how interested Justin Barefoot really was concerning the tranquility of others. Exiting through a low door, the two men passed into a wide conservatory. "What is it you collect?" asked Winston.

"Whatever comes along, Mr. Wyc. If it is of interest to me. I delight, shall we say, in 19th century paintings. Specifically American and English."

Winston wondered if Smelton Castle held any such treasures. The Hudson River School perhaps.

"You have something against historical preservation, Mr. Barefoot?"

Barefoot stopped.

"I'm a strong supporter of conserving our national treasures, Mr. Wyc, when and if they are deserving. My life is spent focused on the past. Smelton Castle was built by a man who history would just as soon forget and unless the Department of Interior suddenly becomes a bureau full of maniacs I doubt if you or anyone could convince them to recognize the property as deserving. It's all a waste of time and money."

Barefoot turned and Winston watched him exit through an arched doorway at the far end of the conservatory. The man was right about the castle. Winston knew before arriving that it had little if any historical importance, but he wasn't going to tell Mr. Conran that until he'd actually seen the place. Maybe he'd be proven wrong. That had not been the case but there were other programs the retreat could pursue if they truly wanted to protect themselves. Although protection seemed up in the air at the moment.

Winston followed Barefoot into a large room fifty

foot square and forty feet high. A marble staircase with a carved stone banister ascended the right wall terminating in another wide mezzanine that overlooked the room. Juliet balconies looked down from the other floors. Wall hangings depicting scenes from the Bible provided color and softened the hard look of the stone walls. On the right, a Palladian doorway led to the outside. Two suits of armor guarded the exit.

"That's the door to the portico," explained Mr. Barefoot.

Winston went to inspect.

"Everyone's in here, Mr. Wyc."

Holding open a door, Justin Barefoot indicated with his expression that Winston should forget the portico.

Taking a deep breath, Winston passed before him and entered the library.

Chapter 3

The library was a long, narrow room lined with glass fronted cabinets. Comfortable leather chairs, each with its own lamp, were spaced about the room. Each a considerate distance from the others, small islands of sanctuary for the recovering oblate. What were they allowed to read? Winston wandered over to study some of the titles.

"Down here, Winston. We've set up a little area for your presentation. Much nicer than the Great Hall. Gentler as it were." Mr. Conran signified where a good place to present might be. Winston wondered about the Great Hall.

At the far end of the room some chairs had been moved into a semicircle facing a fireplace that could have doubled as the mouth of hell in some morality play from the Middle Ages. The marble chimney-piece had been sculpted to show books in various attitudes among which hundreds of tiny fiends molested each other in one way or another. Each standing on a large tome, two four-foot satyrs, their arms raised above their heads, made up the chimney cheeks supporting the mantel, their half grins

24

suggesting more than a quiet read. The original Mr. Smelton must have had an interesting approach to literature, Winston thought as he positioned himself before the small group awaiting him. Moving slightly so that he wasn't standing with his back to the demonic surround, Winston placed his briefcase on the table provided. Besides the festive group Winston had met in the parking lot, he noted an elderly lady sitting in a wheelchair who he supposed was Melody Pinklingill. Sitting just to her left was a short, stocky woman dressed in the habit of a nun, her chubby face spilling out around her constricting headpiece like dough escaping the bread pan. From the center of this fleshy batter two black dots scrutinized Winston with an unnerving intensity. He wondered if she might be the same person he had spotted out in the entrance court earlier. The nun's hand lay on the pushing arm of the wheelchair, her fingers working the frayed leather of the arm in a continuous arc that never varied. Winston found himself staring at the nun's hand and stepped further to his right so that Miss Pinklingill came between him and the nervous motion. Melody Pinklingill, a white-haired, tender looking old lady in a mauve dress, sat studying the wall above Winston's head, her expression bemused and distant. Everyone was seated except Mr. Conran who stood off to the left. The door to the library opened and Ms. Yeats entered quietly, taking a chair well behind those seated before Winston. There to record the session, she held a notepad and pen in her lap.

"Before you begin Mr. Wyc," said Mr. Conran. "I would like to say a few things concerning . . ."

"Michael?"

Everyone turned to look at Melody Pinklingill

who had brought her gaze level with the assembly and was now staring quizzically from Mr. Conran back to Winston.

"Aren't I to be introduced to our guest?"

"Of course you are, Melody, and I was going to do just that, I only wanted to clear the air of some disturbing misconceptions before we started."

"Disturbing . . . ?"

Miss Pinklingill's guard went up. Straining, she rotated her body to face the attendant nun who may have smiled back reassuringly. Winston couldn't be sure. The plump face had appeared to move but it was difficult to discern any positive change in expression among the folds of flesh.

"Well, maybe not disturbing. I've chosen my words badly. There's merely been an oversight on my part that . . ."

"Oversight? Hah!" said Mr. Barefoot loudly.

". . . that has resulted in certain of us . . ."

"I find the word 'disturbing' *quite* appropriate." Mr. Barefoot had stood and was now moving around to the front of the gathering.

"Justin, if you don't mind," said Mr. Conran who moved toward Mr. Barefoot. They both stopped opposite one another directly in front of Winston.

"There is no reason for this man to remain any longer," reported Mr. Barefoot.

"Oh? And why is that?" retorted Mr. Conran.

"Listen, Michael. Don't act the fool. No cause is worth *this*." The two men stared intently at each other. Mr. Barefoot looked away. "Besides, I have talked to Miss Pinklingill and she is not interested in what he has to say."

"I take it then she's here to check out a book," said Mr. Conran, measuring his words.

"I'm sure she's been forced to come here," hissed Mr. Barefoot.

"Miss Pinklingill has come here because she wanted to," said a loud, high voice from behind Mr. Barefoot.

The men turned back to their small audience to find the attendant nun on her feet.

"She would like to be introduced to the gentleman and then have him proceed."

"Thank you," added Miss Pinklingill, nodding.

"Melody!" Mr. Barefoot shot out the name like a cannonball. "When we talked this morning you assured me that that was not the case. You said the offer we've been made was . . . how did you put it? . . . neat-o." Mr. Barefoot rolled his eyes.

"I changed my mind. If only temporarily," she added in a consoling tone.

"You can't do that," said Mr. Barefoot in a strained whisper. He turned on Mr. Conran. "What have you done, you . . . you overblown blue dirigible. What silly promise have you made?"

"You're an ass, Justin."

"You can't say that to Justin." Eric Shrove had joined the fray. "You're a double ass."

"Now wait a minute, Eric."

Reinforcements had joined the Conran camp in the form of Cynthia Shea.

"For goodness sakes. Let's all be quiet." Miss Pinklingill's voice was low but infused with considerable authority. Everyone went silent and looked her way.

"Mr. Wyc, my name is Melody Pinklingill. I understand you have an expertise in a field that we might be interested in knowing more about."

"Happy to meet you. There's no expertise involved

here, Miss Pinklingill, just a passing on of information."

"Perhaps we could hear what you have to say."

"I'd be delighted." Vacationland was beginning to seem light years away. Winston waited as the two gentlemen before him reluctantly took their seats. Miss Pinklingill smiled warmly over her attentive charges. She gave Winston a nod.

"Yes, well . . . let me say first that I apologize for any misunderstandings."

Why am I apologizing, thought Winston.

"Mr. Conran got in touch with me about a month ago concerning the possibility of placing the . . . eh, the retreat on the Registry of Historic Places in Washington. I had him send me a brief history of the castle and some photographs."

I sent him a schedule of my fees, said Winston to himself.

"The procedures involved and the criteria are complicated. We both thought it better if I came here, saw the castle, and talked directly with the board."

"Some of the board," said Mr. Barefoot.

"Some of the board," said Winston softly. "Anyway . . . I should start by saying that the principal reasons for entry are usually places associated with significant events or persons in our history, places that embody . . ." Winston fumbled with his briefcase and his notes. "that embody distinctive characteristics of a type, period or method of construction that represent the work of a master or possess high artistic value . . . *or* are likely to yield information important in history or prehistory for that matter."

"Doesn't sound like Smelton Castle falls under any of *those* headings," snorted Mr. Barefoot.

28

"If Mr. Wyc could just continue . . ." glared Mr. Conran, turning in his chair to get approval from Miss Pinklingill who nodded in Winston's direction.

"There are other considerations, of course. A building with architectural value, a property commemorative in intent, a place closely associated with an important personage . . ."

"How might Smelton Castle rate as historically significant?" asked Cynthia.

"Well, that might be a problem," answered Winston. "I've reviewed a number of . . ."

"Smelton Castle has no historical significance at all, does it, Mr. Wyc?" Mr. Barefoot stood.

"Historical significance . . . no," said Winston.

"But it's such an amazing structure," cried Mr. Conran. "Surely a review board would understand the importance of such an estate. How many castles of this magnitude exist in the United States? Damned few I would think."

"True. It is one of a kind but whether or not it has . . ."

"What Mr. Wyc is too polite to say, Michael, is that the place might make a wonderful theme park but as for its place in American history the verdict is . . ."

"Many an important person visited the castle, Justin. Presidents have stood in this very room and . . ."

"Presidents have stood in a number of places, it didn't make those places historic," Mr. Barefoot jibed.

"What would the board have to do next, Mr. Wyc, and what do you think the real chances of designation might be?" The sensible voice of Cynthia Shea. Winston wanted to hug her.

"I'm not sure how the property would fare, Ms. Shea. The presentation would have to be carefully worded. Although interesting, it doesn't actually fall into any of the categories usually associated with registry, but we could try. The review process can take up to a year and a half."

"A year and a half!" Mr. Barefoot sat back down.

"I personally think the property and the work it does is well worth the time and . . ." Conran was interrupted by Barefoot who stood back up.

"Ridiculous. As *the* major share holder here, I say we vote on the matter. Everyone has a good idea how they feel about the whole thing. I see no reason to drag it out any longer. You have anything else you'd like to say, Mr. Wyc?"

"Not really. There's . . ."

"Good. Let's vote."

"Don't rush it." Conran stood red faced and barely constrained. His body shook.

"I'm with Justin," offered Eric Shrove.

"Who gives a damn," shot back Conran.

"I don't know . . ." said Cynthia. "It is a lot of land. Maybe its importance is environmental instead of historical."

"That's very true. Certainly an avenue to pursue." Conran began rolling up his sleeves. Winston wondered if the man meant to hit someone.

"Hogwash," said Barefoot.

"If I might inject a note of sanity here . . ." said Miss Pinklingill. "Since it's almost lunch hour, why don't we take a few moments by ourselves and give the idea some quiet consideration? Mr. Wyc has been quite informative and I for one thank him. I believe his message is not encouraging for you Michael, but I would like to think about it. A cooling-off period would be helpful."

"And I think we should vote," demanded Mr. Barefoot. "Why prolong this foolishness? All the board members have received my packet explaining in great detail what Shumway and Associates plan to do and have had plenty of time to digest the material. I say we have a discussion about *that* at this point and forget Mr. Wyc's information. I'd like to vote on this matter this afternoon."

"Sit down, Justin."

"Really, Michael. It's not going to work. Give up the idea."

"You listen to me, Justin. Smelton Castle is important to many people and for reasons that have nothing to do with greed. These grounds are a safe and welcoming haven for many, a retreat from the hurts and anxieties of an uncaring world. It's a . . ."

"Please. I've heard enough." Barefoot collapsed with a loud sigh back into his chair. "It's a haven for the rich when they need to have their hand and libido held. Plenty of money traipses through here, Michael. Why don't you ask one of your hurt and anxiety ridden to make an offer? You could name a room or a portion of the garden after . . ."

"Damn it, I'm tired of . . ." Michael seethed.

"It's okay, Michael." The calming voice of Cynthia Shea rose up once again. "Justin has never understood the process of self-surrender to a higher truth. His failure to feel what's true comes from a deep . . ."

"Cut the crap, Cynthia. I forgive myself every night before I go to bed. I don't need you or Michael or anyone to do it for me. This pop psychology number you two have . . ."

"That's enough!" Against the blue cowl, Conran's face looked critically scarlet. "You sit down in Georgetown ooohing and aaahing over your damn paintings while the rest of us . . ."

Winston moved away from the concerned voices and over to the cabinets lining the walls. *The Education of Henry Adams* seemed to be the most arousing title he could find. No one but Miss Pinklingill's nun and Ms. Yeats seemed to notice his slow movement toward the exit. Books nearer the door appeared more the type for the retreat clientele interested in nonfiction: *How to Find Happiness in Foreclosure,* that sort of thing. Behind him the name-calling was reaching uninteresting heights. Winking at Ms. Yeats, Winston stepped from the room. Should he go up the stairs or explore behind one of the other doors that led off the hall?

Two steps at a time, he ascended the staircase. At the top of the stairs his way was blocked by a chain supporting a brass sign that read private. Stepping over the chain, Winston studied the hall to his left and then his right. A door stood open to his left at the end of the hall. Winston strolled casually in that direction, admiring the carved, walnut paneling that lined the hallway. Peeking in and seeing no one, Winston entered a long, narrow, windowless room whose usefulness seemed merely to connect one part of the castle to another. The room was dimly lit and as he moved toward the far end Winston noticed evenly spaced dots of light along the wall to his right. Upon inspection he realized that they were peepholes that looked down into a large room on the floor below. Possibly the Great Hall that Conran had referred to, for it was immense and not all of it was visible from any one hole. Winston heard movement out in the hallway. Leaning back and peeking out, he could see Miss Pinklingill's attendant nun hurrying along from the right and back down the stairs. If and when she had come up the stairs, Winston didn't know; maybe she was looking for him. Coming back into the hall he could hear the nun's hard heels on the stone floor below and then a door shut. Passing by the stairway, Winston explored the hall to the right which ran along for fifteen feet and then took a sharp right turn. There were eight closed doors down this hall, four to the left, four to the right. Winston cautiously opened the one on the left at the end of the hall realizing that it should be directly above the library.

A smaller version of the library below, the room had open shelves along one wall, while on the other, mullioned windows looked out and down on the river view below. Here the furniture was worn and well-used. An overstuffed Chesterfield sofa sat opposite a demon-free fireplace. Several chairs were placed about the room, drawn to a certain spot, used and left there. A long, narrow table stood under a window. Its surface scattered with personal possessions: a framed photograph of a young woman standing in front of a palm tree, a thatch roofed cottage in the background; a pocket watch showing the wrong time; a belt buckle and an ashtray with a freshly snubbed cigarette still smoking in its center. Winston looked about him but the room was empty. Had the nun come up to have a quick smoke? Seemed unlikely, although he hadn't seen anyone else leave. Opening a door next to the sofa, Winston looked into a closet. Several nuns' habits hung from a pole, a number of gray wimples hanging from pegs above them. Perhaps this was the nuns' dressing room.

33

Were the nuns fake or real? Were there such things as freelance nuns? He'd have to ask.

Winston drew aside the white, linen curtain drawn across a window. The casing was eighteen inches deep and Winston had to lean way forward to peer from the window. From this perspective the river looked more like Hudson Lake, its coming and going blocked by massive oaks. Once again a Winston foray into the countryside wasn't going well. Obviously he had been brought up here to turn the head of Miss Melody Pinklingill toward the Conran way of thinking. From the little he had heard, one side wanted to sell the property, the other wanted to make sure it would never be sold. The land must be worth a fortune at this point, reasoned Winston. Could Mr. Conran be that concerned with delivering the weary to the fair shores of Smelton cove? Movement below brought Winston's gaze to the lawn. Mr. Conran's wide back could be seen hurrying away from him. The man slammed a fist into his palm and then, taking a left, veered out of sight around a blue spruce. To his surprise Winston then saw Melody Pinklingill, leaning into the wind, being hurried along the walk that ran before the portico. He watched until she and her attendant nun disappeared behind a wall of rhododendrons. A door slammed. Voices could be heard. A person's footsteps clambered on the stone floor of the entrance hall. Silence.

Winston waited in the hall but the scenario below seemed to be played out. He half expected someone to come up the stairs looking for him or for sanctuary in private surroundings; to flop down on the Chesterfield and rue the day. No one showed. Winston went into the room opposite him.

This room was smaller and almost completely bare except for a cot by the wall and some cardboard boxes taped closed. The cot appeared to be unused. A narrow door opened onto one of the Juliet balconies that overlooked the foyer. The balcony was not deep enough to stand on so Winston leaned out on his elbows to inspect the floor below. Cynthia Shea stood before the main door talking in a low voice to a vigorously nodding Eric Shrove and a sullen Justin Barefoot. Suddenly the little man turned and headed off for the conservatory arch, his eager footfalls receding toward the reception area. Barefoot and Cynthia remained. Winston tried to hear their conversation but was too far above them. Suddenly Barefoot turned and headed out the main door and onto the portico. Cynthia watched after him, standing there looking indecisive.

"Romeo, oh Romeo. Wherefor art thou Romeo?" Winston couldn't help himself.

Startled, Cynthia took a moment to locate Winston's head beaming down on her. Instantly she started up the stairs.

"Mr. Wyc!"

They met at the top of the staircase.

"Mr. Wyc, you are not supposed to be up here. This part of the castle is not open to the public."

"I'm sorry. I didn't realize I was public."

"You know exactly what I mean." Cynthia took a second to catch her breath. "We all were wondering where you'd gone to."

"How did the vote go?" asked Winston.

"Vote . . . ? You're a bit of a card, aren't you Mr. Wyc?"

"I tend to see the humor in things. And please, call me Winston."

35

"Uh huh."

Cynthia began descending the stairs. Winston followed.

"Well actually we decided to break for lunch. Cool out for a short period and try again, that is, if you'd be willing to stay a little longer than planned. If you could, Winston. Maybe you'd like to join Mr. Conran and me for a sandwich."

"I can stay for a while but not too long. And if it's okay with you, I'll lunch alone. I'd just as soon not seem to be taking sides. Maybe I'll take a stroll about the grounds."

"Yes . . . that might be wise."

"To take a stroll?"

"No, no. To lunch alone. Things, if you hadn't noticed, are edgy."

"No kidding. Maybe you could give me a private tour after the meeting adjourns?" he asked.

"I'll ask Michael. I think he has some time after the meeting and he certainly knows the castle much better than I do." She gave Winston a curt, final sort of smile.

Wasn't exactly what Winston had in mind. Cynthia had spoken to him over her shoulder as she moved toward the conservatory.

"When should I reappear in the library?" he called.

Stopping in the arch, Cynthia paused to think. "Say . . . in about forty-five minutes. See you then." A sensible smile and she was gone.

Mission accomplished, he supposed. She had convinced him to stay longer and now it was off to lunch with Michael. Remembering the retreating Conran, Winston hadn't got the impression that the man was particularly interested in eating and he was certainly headed in the wrong direction. Reaching in his pocket, Winston pulled out the crumpled brochures taken from the refectory table earlier. One showed a cursory map of the castle and most of the grounds. Winston would start outside while the sun was still hot on the grass. Breathe in some of that deadly country air.

Chapter 4

Standing on the front portico, Winston surveyed the grounds. His arms outstretched, fingers clutching the stone balustrade, he raised his eyes to the far side of the river. "Someday son . . ." said Winston turning to the imaginary boy on his left, ". . . this will all be yours. *If* you eat your asparagus vinaigrette."

Close to the porch grew enormous rhododendron bushes, the dull green leaves sprinkled with the cerise of fallen petals. The well tended lawn was dotted here and there with beds of annuals, perfect circles of color. At the perimeter, cedars and spruce; behind that, tall oaks and maples. Two hundred yards from the house, the green appeared to vanish, dropped-off like water over a falls. From this angle the Hudson River wasn't visible and the sudden disappearance of lawn had an ominous feel. Poised at this drop was Justin Barefoot, his hands clasped behind him. His head tilted upward, gently turning, matching the circles of a hawk above him. Coming down from the porch, Winston started across the lawn. As cantankerous as Barefoot seemed, he liked the man and even if their styles might be different, Winston saw a person like himself who not only had a great regard for the past but was capable of differentiating between what was historically important and what was not. Not that Winston couldn't still indulge occasionally in what might be called a nostalgia for the past. But when all was said and done, history—for him, and he was sure, for Barefoot—was a business. Conran on the other hand was like many of Winston's clients who used the idea, the sentimentality of history, to preserve what was important to them for reasons that had nothing to do with preservation.

As Winston neared the end of the lawn, Barefoot suddenly stepped off to his left and disappeared over the edge. Alarmed, Winston ran the rest of the way. Upon reaching the rim he had to laugh at himself. There could be nothing less frightening than the gentle slope to the river's edge and beyond . . . Winston caught his breath. Any feelings of menace were quickly dispelled by the magnificence of the panorama. From horizon to horizon, the Hudson River cut the world in half, doing so with authority and grace. Here was a feeling of new frontiers, of uncut woods, of land never walked upon. Winston experienced that sensation of being the first man to stand on a spot. So emphatic was the view that even man's industrial energies, which were evident everywhere, did nothing to diminish it. Such scenery of power lent itself to the contemplation of more weighty human concerns and Winston could see why the banks of the Hudson had been picked by the previous century's robber barons as the site for their weekend cottages. This would have been a purifying vista for even the most self-important of business men who, sitting before their grand homes, sensed the insignificance of their own dominion when compared to the overwhelming authority of nature's power and morality.

Yeah, right, mused Winston. Probably gave all the help an extra two bucks a month and the chamber maid pregnancy leave.

At the water's edge, Winston could just make out the roof of what must be the boathouse. It too had a mansard roof ringed with a parapet and corbeled turrets, the coned tops of which were just visible.

But where had Barefoot gone? Starting along the edge, Winston looked for a way down. After a few yards he spied a path that led downward for a short distance, then disappeared into a thick grove of juniper and cedar. Barefoot must have gone that way. Putting out his arms, Winston was about to plunge over the side when he heard his name called. Turning, he saw Michael Conran huffing toward him along the rim to his left.

"Winston, Winston . . ."

Conran stopped to catch his breath. Winston thought he detected the savory aroma of scotch on Conran's exhales.

"Where are you going?"

"I thought I might take a look at the river. I've read that it's been declared clean up this far."

"It's true." Conran finally eased into a steady rhythm of breathing. "The environmentalists have done a wonderful job of cleaning up the Hudson. Fish are back and once again we can swim its waters, I think."

"You mean the Oblates don't take advantage of the waters for exercise."

"Good heavens, no." For an instant, Conran pinched his large face into a mask of abhorrence. "Our clients might use the river as a metaphor,

Winston, possibly a totem, but never as a recreational tool."

Might get snagged on a figure of speech smiled Winston.

"That's nice. You didn't happen to see which way Mr. Barefoot went. I saw him go over the edge a moment ago but now I seem to have lost him."

"Mr. Barefoot?" Conran looked concerned that Winston might be leaning toward the enemy camp.

"I thought I might be able to convince him to look with more sympathy on land preservation."

"Well, yes . . . yes, that's a good idea. He can be very stubborn, particularly where money is concerned. Yes . . . well, I'm afraid I haven't seen him. Are you sure he came this way?"

"Positive. I was just behind him."

"Justin didn't go by me so he must have taken that path down. It will be time to resume our meeting soon. You will be staying, I hope."

"For a while, yes."

"I'm really appalled at what has occurred today, Winston. You must accept my apology. If I'd had any idea this was going to happen. . . . Have you eaten yet?"

"Not yet. Look, I'd better hurry. I'll bring Justin back with me. Who knows, maybe I'll convince him to go along with your idea."

"Possibly. Be careful, that path's awfully steep."

The path was indeed steep and Winston had to lean back, taking short, choppy steps to negotiate the descent. Twice he had to grab a sapling to steady himself. There must be another way, he thought. I'm going to need a rope ladder if the hill gets any steeper. And then the path disappeared.

It took Winston a few minutes to find where the

path started up again under some low junipers. He was having a hard time believing that Justin Barefoot could have come this way when suddenly the ground leveled out and Winston could walk upright again. Although the undergrowth was still thick, it thinned out at intervals and at each new opening the river had drawn nearer, wider and more vibrant. At the top of the slope, the river had appeared static, unmoving. This close, its strong flow was animated with swirling eddies and cross-currents. The opposite bank looked much farther, more unreachable. For Thomas Smelton to think he could swim the width was unbelievable to Winston.

The path appeared to end again and the remaining fifteen feet to the river was very steep and overgrown with dense shrubbery and brambles. While deciding how to negotiate the incline, Winston thought he heard someone cry out just below him and to his left.

"Mr. Barefoot? Is that you?"

Winston listened. Someone was walking in the brush below him but he couldn't see through the undergrowth. Holding onto a bush, Winston began a cautious descent of the steep embankment. Almost instantly he began to slide and suddenly the earth came out from under him, hurtling him down the hill in a tumbling mass of arms and legs. By the time he reached the bottom he had collected a number of branches and brambles. Winston lay there for a moment, inspecting the various leaves attached to his clothes and mentally checking his body for broken bones. Rising slowly, he carefully picked off the brambles, trying not to collect any more scratches.

He had landed onto a wide path that ran beside the riverbank. Checking along the shore he could see the boathouse a hundred and fifty feet to his left. A hundred feet to his right the path led to a stone outcropping that held two picnic tables. A scenic place to enjoy a metaphor. No sign of Barefoot though. The cry he had heard had been to his left. Maybe Barefoot was at the boathouse.

A piece of floating debris caught his attention. It had risen in the water, shone white in the sunlight and then sank. Winston took two steps and stopped. One of those plastic gloves he assured himself. No reason to think it was actually a hand. Out on the river a pleasure craft had passed sending toward shore a rolling wave of water. Its approach was signaled first by slapping noises on the shore, then more agitated water. Reaching the land, it did a diver's turn and came up ten feet out as a burst of white spray bringing with it Justin Barefoot. There was no mistaking the high brow, the long nose and the haughty mouth formed into a perfect "O" of surprise.

Winston stared, incapable of movement. A quick glance up and down the river provided no clues or assistance. The boat's wake was now bringing the body back to shore. It would sink out of sight, rising closer each time it surfaced. Winston was moving before he actually was aware of moving. A fallen branch appeared in his hand, its crooked end digging at the water, trying to snag the floating Mr. Barefoot. Finally catching the cuff of the man's suit, Winston maneuvered the body backwards until he could reach down and grab the left shoe, its patent leather even shinier in the wet. Dragging the body half up on the shore, Winston had a sudden, involuntary urge to reach down and lift the head out of the water. To keep it from drowning, he realized. Falling back, Winston lay for a moment watching the upper torso bob in the river while he caught his breath and calmed himself. This *was* insane. The last time he had ventured into the countryside he had discovered a dead man. That one had been murdered. Was history repeating itself? Was this his lot each time he left the city? To find dead people? That episode had resulted in him nearly getting murdered himself. New York was the murder capital of the United States and he had to go out into the country to find his share of mayhem. Didn't seem quite fair.

Securing Mr. Barefoot so that he wouldn't slide back into the Hudson, Winston directed his wobbly legs up the shore toward the boathouse hoping there might be someone there or at least a phone.

The boathouse reflected the feudal conviction of the estate, being a mini-castle built out over the water. Four towers joined by fieldstone walls capped by battlements made up the simple structure. The only windows were arrow loops near the top of the towers. Probably to protect the boats from attack by uninvited weekenders, thought Winston. Halfway down the wall on the river side a walled deck had been added that jutted out over the boat entrance to the house. Winston could see the stern section of a large boat anchored on the north side of this deck. He found the entrance for people on the far side of the boathouse, a staircase built into the wall and going up to the deck.

On this side of the boathouse was a wide dock, half of which was anchored securely on land. While the other half, supported by pontoons, rose and sank with the water's rhythm, the large boat rising and falling beside it.

Leaning against the top of the stairs, Winston took in a few gulps of air, forcing himself to be bright and adult. An apartment used as a residence led onto the deck. A line tied to a door frame out to a rail support drooped with the weight of a newly washed pair of pants, the legs of which danced a slow sailor's jig in the wind off the river.

Winston's knock brought a mumbled response from inside followed by a long silence.

"Hello?" said Winston.

Suddenly the door swung open and Winston saw before him a man of indeterminate age, as tall as himself but leaner. The man's veins stood so high off his body they threw shadows on his arms and his neck, pushed upward either by the hardness of his muscles or by an inner tension. Had the face not been so narrow and long, it might have been Indian. The cheekbones were high and prominent, the nose strong and bent at the end. The hair was densely white and cropped close. The eyes, two small lights set far back in the head, were like smugglers' lanterns hoping to attract an unsuspecting ship captain to some offshore reef. Winston sensed as he looked into these eyes that not all was as it seemed or should be.

"Yeah?"

"Sorry but I was just walking along the riverbank here and . . . well . . ."

For an instant Winston wondered if maybe he had hallucinated Justin Barefoot's body.

"Are you a guest of the monastery?" asked the man in a low voice, looking ready to deny Winston his desire for a tour of the large motorcraft that rocked beside them.

"No, no. I'm here to . . . offer information." Weren't those Mr. Conran's words? "Look there's a body washed up down there. A . . ."

"Already?" asked the man. His tone guarded.

". . . a Mr. Barefoot, whom I've just met and . . ." Winston stared at the man. "Already?"

"Mr. Barefoot?"

The man was down the stairs and off the dock

hurrying in the direction that Winston had pointed. They both arrived at the body together. The lean man bent to inspect Mr. Barefoot.

"He's drowned," the man said slowly, staring out into the river.

It seemed so obvious Winston could only shrug. The man touched what looked like blood coming from behind Barefoot's head. He rolled the body to look under it.

"Maybe he didn't drown." He looked up at Winston.

Winston leaned over to look. The man might be right. A deep gash ran behind Barefoot's right ear down toward the center of his lower back. Winston's legs became more wobbly.

"Who are you?" The man stood and faced Winston who had just sat. The lanterns of his eyes had gone dark.

"Winston Wyc. I'm here to give a talk on preservation to the board." It sounded so inane.

After a moment the man moved back toward the boathouse.

"My name's Dace. We better call the police. They like murders."

Chapter 5

Mary Bartlett let her eyes wander from the computer screen and drift across the newsroom. All the reporters seemed busy except her, their fingers tapping out journalese on their IBMs. Mary covered local news for the *New Holland Observer* and it had been a slow news day. It had been a slow news week. Ever since the Macaulay trial had ended the previous month, things had been quiet. Mary had been shunted off the front page and back to the area news section which at the moment meant she was covering the county budget proceedings. This was about as exciting as going camping with Marvin Westbury who hovered over her desk at the moment, hoping she might change her mind.

"Forget it Marv. I'd rather have smallpox."

". . . and you know it's not that far. *And* the cabin has two bedrooms so you don't have to worry about . . . you know."

"No, Marv. What's 'you know'?"

Marvin Westbury had the ability to seem wholly attentive to whomever he was talking to, when in reality he was a hotbed of self-interest. It's what made him an inferior reporter. All Marvin's stories read as if his presence was all the story had needed to make it interesting. Mary found herself doing the same thing during interviews with local sports' heroes but that was the extent of it. She hoped. At least she seemed aware of the problem, Marvin obviously had no inkling.

"So what do you say? Look, don't answer now, I'll come back later when you've had a chance to think it over. It'd be one helluva weekend, I can tell you that."

"I'm busy, Marv."

"I can tell. Those budget talks are so exciting you hardly know where to begin."

The phone rang and Marvin picked it up.

"Observer. Who? Yeah just a sec. It's for you."

"Hello. Oh hi, Rolly. What's up?"

Mary came to attention.

"What? When? Holy moly."

Mary stood.

"Of course I won't. Of course I will. Thanks Rolly. What's that? Give me a break, that's highway robbery. Okay, okay. See you in a minute."

Picking up her bag, Mary handed the receiver back to Marvin.

"Sit on this would ya, Marv? Give your brain something to do."

"Where in the hell are you going in such a rush? Hey?"

"Sorry about this weekend, Marv," Mary yelled over her shoulder. "I'm going to be busy with the front page."

As if prayers were really answered, Mary's phone call from Rolly was a godsend. A murder had been committed. And better yet, no one in the media knew about it except her. She had cultivated Rolly for two years now, giving him twenty-five bucks each time he tipped her off as to any celebs seeking R&R down at the monastery. Most tips had never panned out, but all those twenty-five bucks were paying off now. One of the board members had been found facedown in the Hudson and he wasn't doing the crawl. She should check in with Bossman, this being her affectionate sobriquet for her editor in chief Matt Laird, but he might want to send someone from the cop-shop and that wouldn't do at all. She would call him from the monastery with the scoop. Good-bye revenue sharing, hello homicide.

Mary had always driven as if the distance between two points were a big waste of time. So only twenty minutes had passed when she eased her GMC Pacer through the gate of the Oblates of Tranquil Deliverance and pulled up even with the guardhouse. Rolly came bounding out before she'd even stopped. Mary guessed Rolly to be in his fifties, though he could have been a dissipated forty-five. He had the blotchy red face of a drinker and always looked and acted as if he'd eaten too much only moments before you met him.

"What ya got in this thing? A jet engine or what? My phone's still warm." Wiping his brow, Rolly leaned in her window.

"The Pacermobile travels the speed of light when there's a murder in the neighborhood. There *was* a murder?"

"Justin Barefoot, that Southern fella, like I said on the phone. Now don't go telling anyone I told ya, okay. Or my ass is grass."

"Where's this Southern fellow reposing?"

"Reposing? What the hell kind of word is that?"

"Where's he at, Rolly?"

"Down by the river. At least that's where the cops have been heading. Here I was minding my own when suddenly the gate is stuffed with the buggers. What's going on, I ask all innocent. Body down at the boathouse, they say. Conran calls, says let nobody but the cops in." Rolly gave her one of his special winks. "He's the one that tells me it's Barefoot."

"Who's down there?"

"Captain Sweetman and his boys. And Dutch I'm pretty sure."

"He see anything?"

"Don't know. You'll have to ask him yourself."

"Back in the guardhouse, Rolly. Time's a wasting."

"About being paid?"

"Oh yeah." Mary squinted at him and removed a fifty from her shirt pocket. "Bloodsucker."

"And, isn't sweet Mary glad to have the story?"

"You're my favorite informer, Rolly." If this thing panned out she was going to have to keep Rolly in her good graces.

"Claire Yeats on the monitor?" she asked.

"Probably. Park at the first turn around and walk down the back way. I'll get hell later but I turned her off here. I knew you were coming and besides, knowing she's staring at me all the time gives me the willies."

"Thanks Rolly."

Mary parked at the turnaround. From here she could approach the castle without giving herself away immediately. What she was going to do was not quite clear yet. Rolly had said on the phone that the body had been found about forty-five minutes before he called. That was almost thirty minutes ago so that meant an hour and fifteen, hour and half had passed since the discovery. The cops would still be swarming all over the boathouse so she'd have to put off talking to Dutch for a while. Maybe she'd explore the castle first. Mary knew how to enter from the back and not be seen. Rolly had showed her that last summer. If they caught her inside she'd confront them with the story and take it *and* their reaction to the press. The week in local news was definitely looking up.

Chapter 6

Winston sat on the balustrade of the portico watching Cynthia Shea pace back and forth. Every few minutes she would come over to say how she couldn't believe it. Winston had given up verbally agreeing with her and now only shook his head. A Captain Sweetman was presently in the library interrogating Michael Conran. It seemed Winston was to be the last one called, all the others having been interviewed. Melody Pinklingill and her nurse were sitting quietly in the conservatory, while Eric Shrove had been given a sedative and made to lie down. Winston wasn't sure where Mr. Barefoot had wound up, probably waiting in one of the emergency vehicles still down at the boathouse for his ride to the New Holland morgue.

An hour earlier, waiting on the boathouse porch as Dace called the police, Winston had looked out over the river and watched the pleasure crafts dart to and fro. Noisy motorcrafts wove their way in among the silent sailboats. Suddenly the wind would change direction and a laugh or shout, even bits of conversation, could be heard across the water. Happy people oblivious to the dead man hugging the mud only feet from where they enjoyed themselves. Winston wondered if someone on one of those very boats had darted in, struck Justin Barefoot and then, unseen, sped away to the opposite shore. He was having a difficult time believing that any of the people he'd just met might have been responsible. Tempers had been high when he left the library, but none of the other board members impressed him as killers. Winston had been startled by the arrival of the patrol cars. Turning, he had found Dace staring at him from a window and police officers swarming the dock. From then until now, events had unfolded as if in a dream. Taken back to the body, Captain Sweetman had asked a few questions, then Winston had been whisked up to the castle where the others had been herded into the library and informed of the death. At that point pandemonium ruled. It had taken Sweetman and his men many minutes to calm everyone. A doctor was called to administer to Eric Shrove who had fallen apart completely. Except for the occasional officer bounding up the portico steps with information for the Captain, the last hour had been as it was now, a time of tense and anxious silence. For Winston it had been like attending one of those avant-garde plays in which the audience is shuttled from one room to another to spy on brief portions of the play. Disjointed and without exposition, the scenes are unintelligible by themselves and it is not until the denouement that, one hopes, it all begins to make sense. Winston hoped the end was in sight for him.

Conran appeared on the porch with a policeman. The big man looked several inches shorter than the last time Winston had seen him.

"Mr. Wyc?" asked the young officer. "Captain Sweetman would like to talk to you now, sir."

Captain Sweetman stood at the far end of the library staring into the mouth of hell, his elbow resting on the chest of a satyr. It was not until Winston had been seated that he turned. The captain was impeccably dressed; his dark suit well-tailored; a boutonniere of tiny, crimson flowers matching the color of the one thin stripe on his gray tie. Every dark hair was in place, the moustache perfectly trimmed. Although only five-foot-six or seven, the captain was physically impressive, his body well-muscled and toned like a man who spent hours in the gym; the skin on his face tight, almost shiny. Settling into a comfortable stance, the captain didn't move again, his voice carrying all the conversational focus and gesture. At first Captain Sweetman's lack of movement bothered Winston until he realized that if the man actually became animated it was probably time to leave the room. In a hurry.

"What do you think of this fireplace, Mr. Wyc?"

"I beg your pardon."

"Mr. Conran says you're an architectural historian. I thought you might have an opinion." A satyr grinned at Winston over the Captain's shoulder.

"I think it would keep me out of the library in the evenings."

"That's understandable." The captain stared at Winston just long enough for it to be uncomfortable. "I know we talked down at the river, Mr. Wyc, and I might repeat myself but I would like for Officer Bensen to tape us as we talk. Do you mind if we tape our conversation?"

"No." Winston wasn't convinced.

"It won't take long. We used to have someone write these interviews down but I always found that something would not be recorded or would be transcribed incorrectly . . ." the captain trailed off.

Winston turned to find the young policeman who'd brought him in sitting quietly by the window, a portable cassette recorder on the table before him.

"You were here to give a talk or something, Mr. Wyc?"

"Mr. Conran had called me in New York asking me to come to Buddingville and present to the board of the retreat the review process involved for possible entry on the National Register of Historic Places."

"You'd never been here before today?"

"Never."

"Or met any of the board members before today?"

"I'm afraid not."

"Why would they want to be put in the Registry?"

"People have various reasons for wanting to enter. I think in this case it was to protect the land from development."

"Rather than for historical reasons?"

"People think they have history in mind when they call me but many times that's not the case. Usually it's to thwart a developer, stop State expansion or undermine a next of kin. It has nothing to do with whether or not the property in question warrants designation. I think the retreat might have a difficult time in the review process. Although the property is interesting, it doesn't actually have any historic or architectural value. Also, properties owned by religious institutions have a hard time."

"I'd have to look into it, Mr. Wyc but I don't believe the Oblates of Tranquil Deliverance is protected from the tax books by religious designation. It's a business run like a monastery, not the other way around."

"Makes sense. I should have guessed." Winston wished Captain Sweetman would move from in front of the fireplace. Because of his odd lack of physical movement he was beginning to blend into the surround. Just another satyr asking questions.

"Could you go over with me again how you found Mr. Barefoot?"

Winston repeated what he had told the captain standing at the river—his following Barefoot, the descent down the hill, the cry he heard and his chance discovery of the body.

"You say you watched the river from the edge of the lawn. Did you notice anyone?"

"I ran into Michael Conran at the top of the hill. We talked briefly and he headed back toward the castle."

"He mentioned seeing you. What did you talk about?"

"Not much. How clean the river was getting, that sort of thing. I asked him if he'd seen Barefoot. He said he hadn't."

"Did you believe him?"

"I think so. At the time I had no reason to believe he was lying." Winston thought a moment. "I still don't. Conran showed up only minutes after Mr. Barefoot had disappeared over the edge. He couldn't possibly have had anything to do with the . . . the assault on the man."

"He's not being accused of anything, Mr. Wyc."

Winston felt himself redden. "Sorry. I'm starting to play detective."

"That's all right. Everyone does." Sweetman went silent again. After a full minute he spoke. "You didn't spot a boat nearby?"

"I thought about a boat later, but no, I saw nothing. I did . . ." Winston hesitated.

"Yes?"

"Getting back to Conran. I don't know if it's important, but when we met on the hill I could smell liquor on his breath." And I was jealous, Winston thought to himself.

"Mr. Conran had mentioned his going back to his cottage on the estate grounds to have a drink. I think he needed to relax after the argument in the library. What about this argument, Mr. Wyc?"

"There was some disagreement as to the . . . eh . . . the sensibleness of pursuing historical designation. Conran was in favor while Mr. Barefoot was not."

"Everyone has mentioned it. Rather hesitantly, I might add."

Winston nodded.

"Ms. Shea says that you left the library early."

"It's true. Since it had nothing to do with me I decided to explore the castle until they sorted it out. I went upstairs."

"Did you meet anyone?"

"No but I did see Miss Pinklingill's nurse. I think she was looking for me."

"You didn't talk to her?"

"No."

"I see. You didn't notice Mr. Barefoot walk across the lawn then? Or meet anyone."

"No. I saw him in the hallway after the meeting broke for lunch, talking to Eric Shrove and Ms. Shea, but once I got outside he was already at the edge of the lawn."

"By himself."

"By himself."

"How long from the last time you saw Mr. Barefoot did you find his body?"

"Fifteen, twenty minutes. If I hadn't taken that particular path it would have been faster. I might have seen Barefoot's killer. Maybe saved his life."

"Or lost yours."

Winston hadn't thought of that. This was not the

way to start a vacation. He flinched as the Captain suddenly moved toward him.

"Could you go over the argument in the library for me, Mr. Wyc? What was actually said. No one else seems to remember any details."

"There wasn't that much said actually. Barefoot and Conran went at it right from the beginning. I tried to explain the criteria and the procedure involved but they kept interrupting. It seemed personal."

"Did the others get into it?"

Winston mentioned the lineup.

"Barefoot had obviously been made an offer on the property and wanted the board to vote on it. He seemed the only one really eager to sell, though."

"Selling the property would put them all out of the retreat business, wouldn't it?"

"Maybe, but there seems to be plenty of land to me. Why they can't divide it up and sell off a big chunk and keep the retreat at the same time I don't understand. That would be one solution that might satisfy everyone but, I'm afraid, alternatives weren't discussed. Of course it might have something to do with the way the estate is set up. Maybe when Smelton sold it he had covenants of some kind placed in the deed so that the land couldn't be subdivided. Who knows?"

"I shall look into that, Mr. Wyc. It might have a bearing." Sweetman looked over at Officer Bensen.

"I don't know how the retreat is owned Captain, but I got the feeling that each of the board members had bought into the venture. That they all owned a part of it. Barefoot mentioned being the major share holder. You might look into that. I don't think the ownership was equally divided."

"You think Barefoot only needed one or two votes to carry the sale."

"I think so."

"I take it there was never a vote."

"I don't know. I left."

Captain Sweetman thought back over what Winston had told him. "Was there anything interesting mentioned in the name-calling?"

Winston smiled as he thought back. "In the heat of the moment, hey?"

"Something like that. People can say incriminating things when they're angry."

"At one point Barefoot said to Conran that 'No cause is worth this.'"

"No cause? What cause was that, do you think?"

"I took it to mean the bringing of peace to those wealthy enough to pay for it."

Sweetman smiled.

"Thank you, Mr. Wyc. You've been very helpful. I think you might make a very good detective. I shall look into these particulars you've brought up. Oh, one more thing."

"What's that?"

"You implied that the chances for the retreat being granted a historic designation were slim. Had you mentioned this to anyone on the board?"

"I mentioned it to everyone present in the library."

"I see. Well, thanks again. I believe this is yours."

"It is. Thank you."

Handing Winston his briefcase, Sweetman walked with him to the door.

"I realize you live in New York, but I'm afraid I'm going to have to ask you to stick around for another day. I'll need you to sign the typed transcript of the tape and probably to answer more questions. I never seem to get everything the first time."

"I'm supposed to be on vacation," said Winston in a low voice.

The captain pursed his lips, staring at the bookcase over Winston's shoulder.

"Then you wouldn't mind? There's been a murder, Mr. Wyc. You might be my only reliable witness."

Winston could think of nothing to dispute the point.

"I can't really hold you, Mr. Wyc, but I'd appreciate your staying close by. If you can't ..." The captain spread his hands out before him, a very unusual expansive gesture. "...I would understand."

"I hear New Holland's beautiful this time of year."

Grinning, Sweetman held out his hand. "Thanks."

Standing next to a suit of armor in the entrance foyer, Winston stared out at the lawn. He'd have to call the hotel in the city and delay his check in for another day. Maybe the Captain would only need him for tomorrow.

Conran and Cynthia could be seen on the portico talking.

"Hi," said Winston.

"I don't know what to say, Mr. Wyc. I drag you all the way up here and ... now this. If there's anything I can do for you."

Mr. Conran seemed to be genuinely humbled by the event and concerned about Winston's welfare. Cynthia still appeared red faced, drawn and confused.

"A phone. I need to make a call. Long distance if that's all right. Captain Sweetman wants me to hang about for another day. I'm his key witness, it would seem."

"It would probably be helpful if you would. You'll find one back in the reception area where we came in. Ask Claire to help you. You go back through the conservatory ..."

"I can find it."

"Did you see *anything* when you found the body, Mr. Wyc, a person, a weapon, anything that would give you some idea of . . . of anything?" Cynthia was having difficulty keeping control.

"I saw nothing. I'm sorry."

The three stared out at the edge of the lawn.

"I'll make that call now, if that's okay. I'm expected somewhere."

Miss Pinklingill blocked his way as he entered the sun room.

"Mr. Wyc. Might we have a moment of your time."

"Yes?"

"The events of the day are very disturbing as you well know." Miss Pinklingill followed Winston's eyes over her shoulder. "I'm sorry. This is Sister Mary Crosse. Mary is my engine and my albatross."

Sister Mary Crosse nodded at Winston; a slow, gelatinous bobbing of the head. Winston took the spread of the cheeks and the squinting of the eyes to be a smile. The tag "albatross" didn't seem to offend her.

"It's nice to meet you, and please call me Winston. And I'm sorry about Mr. Barefoot. I got the impression the two of you were close."

"We were . . . Winston, but the last few years . . . well, you know . . . with older people it becomes more difficult to get around . . . shall we say."

Winston nodded in agreement. With Mary the Engine behind her, she seemed to get around pretty well.

"I need to ask what might seem a foolish question and I don't want you to think me a foolish woman."

"Of course not."

Miss Pinklingill thought a moment. Although a thin woman in a wheelchair, she appeared strong and in good health, her thinness pleasing and graceful. The eyes shone with intelligence and Winston could feel he was being sized up.

"When you found Justin, was his aspect one of contentment, of peace?"

Winston thought a moment.

"Well, yes, I guess it was. He appeared . . ." Winston resisted using the word "tranquil." "He appeared . . . at peace."

He appeared dead, thought Winston, assuming his best caretaker slump with concerned expression. The few dead people he had ever seen all looked the same: abandoned, hollow, blank.

"I see. It's important, Winston . . . to know. As you draw nearer the end it becomes important."

"I think I understand."

Winston didn't understand at all and the three stared off into their separate voids, reasoning out the unexplainable. Winston cleared his throat.

"If you'll excuse me I have to make a phone call. Captain Sweetman wants me to spend the night and I must tell my office."

"Oh, good. Then you'll stay. I still want to learn about saving history, Winston. It's something I'd like to care about. Possibly we could meet later."

Winston assured Miss Pinklingill that he wouldn't leave without informing her of his expertise and fled the room. Sister Mary's pinprick eyes were beginning to disturb him. The whole situation was disturbing him. Maybe he wouldn't call the Sherry-Netherland at all. Would the Oblates think less of him if he sped away in his rented Cougar, never to return? Sweetman had said he couldn't rightfully hold him. Slipping back down the corridor, Winston thought of Justin Barefoot and his collection of nineteenth century paintings. Did he have a family waiting for him back in Virginia? What could he possibly have done or known to get himself killed?

The reception area looked the same: dark and uncomfortable. What a dismal welcome for anyone ready to be delivered. The outside held such promise. He knocked on Ms. Yeats's open door.

"Oh, hi. Come in. What can I do for you?"

Ms. Yeats sat nonplussed at her desk among her papers, glancing up occasionally at the four security monitors that were mounted on the opposite wall, eating a sandwich.

"You Claire? Mr. Conran said to ask you for a phone."

"I'm Claire."

"Pretty name." A little flirting wouldn't hurt Winston decided.

"It sucks. You can use that desk over there. Is it a private call?" This was said with exaggerated concern.

"Not really." Maybe flirting wasn't such a hot idea. "I have to put off an arrival. Seems I'm staying in Buddingville tonight."

"Yeah? Will you be here at the monastery?"

Winston had given no thought to his sleeping arrangements for the night. The monastery would not have been his first consideration. People got killed here.

"I don't know."

"I see." Claire took a big bite of her sandwich. "Isn't it terrible about Mr. Barefoot?"

"Terrible," echoed Winston. The woman might have been talking about the weather.

"And you found the body. What a bitch. That'd ruin my week, I can tell you."

Winston dialed New York.

"Hello, the Sherry-Netherland, my name is Win-

63

ston Wyc. I have a room reserved for the night. Uh huh. That's right, the whole week. Look . . . I need to cancel for tonight. Something beyond my control has come up. There's a what? Hmmm. Well okay. Yeah, the rest of the week is still on. I understand that. See you by four o'clock tomorrow. Thanks."

Winston watched Claire as he talked. She didn't seem interested in what he was saying, only in eating her lunch and staring at the monitors, one of which was dark.

Cradling the receiver, Winston placed his head in his hands. He was getting that wobbly feeling back, that tingling sensation in the back of his head. The events of the afternoon were catching up to him. The last place in the world he wanted to be was Buddingville.

"Thanks for the phone. Think I'll take a breath of fresh air. We don't get much of it down where I come from."

Claire was trying to wipe tuna fish off a manila folder and barely looked up. "Anytime."

Winston stood outside in the courtyard wishing his legs would get with the program. There's nothing more crippling than trauma-sensitive patellas. Taking in a few deep breaths he considered his next move. The high walls of the castle now seemed more penal than medieval and the urge to explore had been dampened. A place to stay was going to be needed. The retreat would not be his first choice but he wasn't sure the travel account provided for rooms at the local Ramada Inn. As he was wondering if Cynthia stayed at the retreat, someone moved next to him. Turning, Winston was surprised to see a tall, slender woman with a crew cut coming toward him. Although dressed in jeans and a T-shirt, her manner suggested all business. A red silk scarf tied loosely around her neck gave accent to the short, black hair. Shifting an oversized brown bag from one hip to the other, the woman settled her willowy frame beside him, giving him a blunt, appraising look. The short haircut, disturbing on many women, worked wonderfully here to accent the large, black eyes and the high, full cheeks. The thoughtful mouth spread suddenly into a wide smile.

"Hi," she greeted.

"Hi. You come with the monastery or the police?"

"Neither. I'm a reporter for the *New Holland Observer*."

"Oh great."

"I knew you'd be thrilled. I'm Mary Bartlett."

Winston reluctantly shook the offered hand.

"I'm Winston Wyc."

"Wick? Like the air freshener?"

"W.Y.C. Like Wycowski."

"Polish."

"That's right. My grandfather was under the impression a non-Polish sounding name would fare better in the new world, so he shortened it."

"Wyc? That name rings a bell for some reason. You from around here?"

"Nope."

"You up from New York then?"

"You mean today or originally?"

"Both."

"Yes to the above."

"And you're a guest?"

"Not at all. I was invited up here to look at the Smelton estate and deliver a sermon on review procedures."

"What for?"

"Why do I feel I'm part of an old 'Dragnet' TV episode."

"I wouldn't know. I hear there's been a murder and you found the body."

"I . . . wait a minute. How come you know so much? Have I been compromised by some tiny hearing device?"

Winston pretended to pat himself down. Mary laughed.

"I happen to overhear your conversation with Claire. I was standing out in the reception area eavesdropping. Hey, don't look so taken aback. It's a dog-eat-dog, anything goes, media-gone-mad world out there. One must learn how to survive."

"By sneaking around?"

"By being on top of things. So what's the story? You find this guy or what?"

"I don't believe I can comment on that," Winston said with a smile. Mary smiled back.

"But you can. It's expected of every American to support free press and the dissemination of accurate and unbiased reporting. How am I to do that if you clam up?"

"Do what every other reporter does—fake it."

"Such cynicism. You hungry? I'm starving. Come on, I'll buy you a pizza you'll swear was made in the City."

Taking Winston's arm, Mary began guiding him toward the back exit. Winston was glad to follow.

"What kind of review procedure we talking here?" she queried.

"I'm an architectural historian."

"What kind of animal is that?"

Michael Conran stopped them from the door.

"Hello! What in the hell are you doing here? No one here called the paper."

Mr. Conran was not pleased to see the *New Holland Observer* represented at the retreat. They'd had their run-ins with this young lady before. Mary didn't miss a beat.

"Come to see my old friend, Winston. We went to school together way back when. P.S. 254. In the City." Again the big smile, the large bag shifted to the front, a barrier against attack.

Mr. Conran gave Winston a questioning look.

"Small world, huh?" said Winston.

"I doubt if you've ever been out of New Holland, Ms. Bartlett. Captain Sweetman would be very upset if he knew you were here. I know he wishes the events of the day to remain within the confines of the monastery walls. If you don't mind?"

"What events are those?" asked an innocent Mary Bartlett looking from Conran to Winston.

"Look . . . eh, Mary. Maybe we should hold off on the pizza until later." Like next week.

A cloud passed over Mary's face.

"I think that's a wise decision, Winston," declared Conran.

Winston considered changing his mind if only to remove Conran's smug look.

"Well, look Winston, since you get to spend the night maybe a little later would be better," said Mary.

Conran had turned to see who was approaching from the reception area and Mary bared her teeth at Winston in a fake snarl.

"You don't miss a thing, do you?" said Winston in a low voice.

"Not much," Mary answered under her breath. Then loudly, "By the way, where *are* you spending the night, old buddy?" Mary shifted the bag back to her left hip.

Cynthia Shea came out the door to stand next to Conran.

"What is she doing here?"

Popular young lady, thought Winston. All this hostility was a plus in her favor as far as he was concerned. Maybe he should spend some time with Mary. Seek refuge. Try and talk her out of any sensational headlines.

"A friend of Winston's, or so she says," said Conran.

"We go back forever," Mary beamed at Cynthia.

Cynthia took a moment to assess the situation, her eyes moving back and forth from Winston to Mary.

"Is this true, Mr. Wyc?"

"Our fathers were butchers in the same shop back in Brooklyn," said Winston giving Mary a wry look. Mary managed to beam even broader at Cynthia.

"Where *am* I going to spend the night?" Winston thought he better change the subject.

"You should stay here, of course," said Conran. "We feel greatly responsible for what has happened."

"What was that?" asked Mary, again the very embodiment of innocence. Conran ignored her.

"You will join us . . . Winston."

More a statement than a question, Winston nodded hesitantly and shrugged.

"We really must talk, Winston," said Conran. "Maybe you could call your friend later this evening."

"Why don't you do that . . . eh, Winston. Here's my number . . . in case you forgot to bring it." Mary turned to Conran and Cynthia. "I happen to know there's been a murder here this afternoon. Anyone here like to comment on that?"

Conran and Cynthia looked at each other in horror.

"Winston, I don't think it's a good idea to go around . . ."

"It wasn't me. Mary already knew."

"How did you know?" Conran was getting quite red. "Did someone from the monastery call?"

"Then it's true. Someone was killed."

"No comment and I think you should leave right now."

"It might be better for you to issue some kind of statement then to have me print a hostile story. I know about the murder and tomorrow so will everyone else. I bet there's twenty cops running around this place and each one's going to tell somebody. There's the people at the morgue, there's the . . ."

"Okay, you've made your point." Conran shook his head at Cynthia. "Maybe we should go back inside. I'll have Claire type something up. Would you mind waiting in the reception area until it's done and then I want you off the property."

"Thanks. Winston and I can stay out here if that's okay."

"I would just as soon you waited inside."

"It's okay, Mr. Conran," said Winston. "I won't say anything about the incident. I'd like to stay in the fresh air."

"Fine. I'll go in and dictate something to Claire. It won't take a minute." Conran leaned over and whispered to Cynthia who remained behind as Conran disappeared back into the building.

"I don't believe I heard your name, Ms . . ."

"Bartlett."

"I'm Cynthia Shea. You'll excuse Mr. Conran, Ms. Bartlett. He's had a bad day. This whole affair has been quite a shock to all of us. You understand."

"Certainly."

"How did you find out?"

"Purely a coincidence. I live just down the river

69

and was walking along the shoreline and came upon the police. Having been on the police beat for the paper, I know many of the men."

"Oh."

The three stood in silence until Conran reappeared waving a sheet of paper.

"Here you are. I phoned Captain Sweetman down at the boathouse and he said it was all right."

Mary scanned the typewritten page. "Always glad to get the captain's approval."

"Now, if you don't mind." Folding his arms, Conran lifted his chin in the direction of the gate.

"Sure. Thanks for the information." Mary turned to Winston with one of her wide grins. "Call me. You people stay in touch."

Giving her bag a toss, Mary followed it into the parking lot. All three stood watching as she exited through the brick archway.

"I'd like to know how she found out," said Conran.

Cynthia related what Mary had told her.

"Where down the river could she live? She drove past the guardhouse more than likely. I noticed Roland's monitor was dead again. That man's walking on thin ice. Maybe it's time to have a long talk with our security." Conran eyed Winston. "So you and this woman go back to high school, Winston?"

How long should I let this go on, thought Winston. It's pretty clear the two of us had never met and yet . . .

"We weren't very close at all," said Winston shaking his head. "At all."

"Oh well. I'm glad you're staying the night, Winston. We have only a skeleton crew during the week, most of our deliverees being weekenders. Except for the staff I'm here by myself tonight. Not a pleasant thought."

Winston wasn't sure yet that he wanted to stay at the retreat. "What about Eric Shrove?" asked Winston wondering why Conran didn't want to spend the night alone. Conran certainly didn't need Winston to hold his hand.

"Miss Pinklingill has offered to accommodate Eric. If he ever wakes up. The poor man was a mess."

"She lives elsewhere?"

"Melody lives in Buddingville," piped in Cynthia. "I have a house north of New Holland. At the foot of the Catskills. Lovely."

"I can imagine."

The three stood in the reception area staring at the arched doorway as if expecting someone. Suddenly wishing he had left with Mary Bartlett, Winston had a horrifying vision of himself and Conran spending the whole evening standing about the refectory table discussing nothing in particular. Or worse, discussing the castle's chances of historical designation. Perhaps he'd take a drive or wander the halls or . . . or go back to the City. Others kept taking for granted that he was going to stay at the retreat that night. He only wanted to return to the West Village where he lived and finish the latest Sue Grafton, *K is for Keeps*. Much better to read about a murder than to be involved in one. Winston was not interested in staying in a dark, dank, fifty room castle with no change of clothes, no toiletries, no good reason to stay and a very good chance of having an encounter with a homicidal maniac. Bring on the nuns.

"What's behind all the doors?" Winston tried to sound interested.

71

"This area was originally the delivery entrance," said Conran. How appropriate thought Winston. "To the left was the scullery and beyond that the kitchen. Three of the doors enter into large closets used to store things as they arrived. We keep bicycles in them now, that sort of thing. The others lead to different parts of the castle. We now use two of the rooms as offices and a third as a small conference room. The servants' quarters were directly above us and reached through that door there. Board members or special guests stay in the rooms off the mezzanine up there. I'm afraid since Justin was in one of those rooms that area is off-limits at the moment."

"Perhaps Mr. Wyc would like to see his room for the night. Settle in a little," Cynthia suggested. "Maybe you could then show him the castle. You'd have time before dinner."

"Excellent idea. What do you say, Winston?"

"Sure but you know I can stay elsewhere if it's a problem."

"No problem at all. I'd love the company."

Winston was almost touched, but not quite.

"Thanks."

"Michael, I must be going. I'll call later around six."

Any indication of Cynthia's previous anguish was gone, Winston noted, watching her straighten her hair with her hands and a little toss of the head, the sensible smile firmly back in place.

"Fine. Talk to you then." His own smile lurking just below the surface, Conran watched Cynthia leave.

"A beautiful woman, Winston."

Hoping his half smile wasn't altogether sleazy, Winston nodded. Taking in a deep, healthful breath,

Conran clicked his heels together and with a flourish indicated the correct way to Winston's room.

"If you'll follow me, please."

Winston felt as if he were being gallantly led off to the tower from where he could sit and watch the guild carpenters construct his gallows. He swore a private oath that he would never leave New York City again.

Chapter 7

Making her way along the tree line that led down to the boathouse, Mary considered what she knew about Justin Barefoot. She had once met the man at a fund raiser for Frederick Church's estate, Olana. She remembered him as a tall gentleman, pinched and patrician in demeanor, much interested in the Hudson River School of painting. In fact, she recalled that he waxed rather eloquent about the American landscapists of that period. Of how they captured the romantic and savage nature of the land, a perfect metaphor for a burgeoning America. Burgeoning had been his word, though certainly not his style. He had been reserved, almost snobbish, and as she remembered he was adamant about *not* having a story published in the paper concerning his interest and his collection. Later she had discovered from a local artist that Barefoot had cut a deal with the retreat people to invest a large sum of money if he got all the Hudson River School paintings hanging in Smelton Castle, a sizable if not particularly celebrated group of pictures. There had been a stink among local historians concerning his taking the paintings to somewhere in the South. Where, exactly

Mary couldn't remember. Maybe some deranged art historian had acted out belated revenge on Barefoot's thievery.

Speaking of historians. That Winston Wyc was certainly a cutie. The poor man hadn't seemed particularly excited about staying at the monastery. Maybe she should get back to him and offer him a place to stay. New Holland was limited in its selection of eligible men, and although Mary wasn't interested in settling down, she was tired of men who thought she should be. Winston didn't strike her as the type ready to meet any in-laws and besides he hadn't given her away to that Conran bastard. Maybe she could convince him to stay a few more days.

And what was this historian doing at the monastery? She'd have to find out more about this review process. Even if the reason had nothing to do with the murder it might be interesting in itself. As they taught in Journalism 101, leave no source unturned.

Mary stepped into the trees to avoid being hit by the morgue van as it passed up the drive. She had seen this vehicle before but never with any crime victims inside. Painted black, with dark windows, the word morgue printed in small gold letters on the doors, the van had always struck Mary as the embodiment of despondency and gloom. Usually its interior held casualties of poverty, abuse or shame, never the wealthy victims of homicide. Not in New Holland. The well-to-do had better methods of censuring their own. A name dropped from the invitations, no morning chats over the phone lacerating others, children suddenly no longer available as playmates. This system was much deadlier than the knife or club. The victim of murder was safely beyond the weak smile, the ingratiating snub. Too easy an out. Of course, Justin Barefoot was from another planet as far as the locals were concerned. Unless it had been an unfortunate misadventure, Barefoot's killer would almost certainly have to be someone at the monastery.

The boathouse looked like a small castle under siege. It was surrounded by emergency vehicles, their rotating lights attacking the walls with hostile blues and reds. Pinning her press card to her shirt, Mary took a deep breath and bolted forward, her stride bold and confident. Best to appear as if she had been invited. Sergeant Jones stopped her as she passed his patrol car.

"Hey Mr. Bartlett! Where the hell do you think you're going?"

"Oh hi, Sarge, that's *Ms.* Bartlett to you. Catch the killer yet?"

Jones leaned forward, squinting his eyes. "Well, I'll be, if it isn't sweet Mary. Hey, I'm sorry, I thought you were a boy. Must have been the way you walk, eh."

"Must be, Sarge. The body still down by the river?"

"And what body would that be?"

"No body, huh? Then you won't mind if I just take a little stroll down . . ."

"Hold on, *Ms.* Bartlett, you stay right where you are. No one's allowed past here. And where's Harris? I thought he had the honors of following the cops around."

"He's on sabbatical. I'm filling in." Mary offered one of her wide smiles. Sergeant Jones was obviously confused as to what Harris might be up to. "Besides, what difference does it make?"

"None, I guess, but you have to stay on this side of the dock. Captain's orders. The forensic boys haven't finished going over the area yet. Wouldn't want anyone messing up clues."

Mary glanced over at the cops milling back and

forth on the river path, oblivious to the area around them or to the possibility of destroying evidence.

"I can see it might be a problem. Where is the Captain?"

"He just went down to the body. The morgue guys are wrapping him up now."

On cue, four men came up the path carrying a stretcher, their burden zipped into a dark body bag. Mary shuddered as they went past her. No matter how tough she considered herself, dead people were always disturbing. She didn't like being reminded of her own vulnerability. Following the stretcher was Captain Sweetman talking to a young officer on his right. Upon seeing Mary, the Captain broke off his conversation and headed in her direction.

"Hello, Ms. Bartlett."

"Hi Captain. Anything for the *New Holland Observer?*"

"Possibly. Didn't Conran give you some information. I talked to him over the phone. I think he was upset to find you in his backyard."

"Nah. Mr. Conran and I are like family."

Sergeant Jones laughed behind her. "If you're anything like my family that's no special deal."

"What is it you'd like me to add to Conran's statement?"

Mary took a folded sheet of paper out of her bag.

"This just mentions when the man was killed and some history on him. How he died would be nice to know and whether or not you have any suspects."

"Mr. Barefoot was struck from behind and fell into the water. At least that's the way it appears at the moment. We'll know more in a few days. As for suspects, I wish I could say."

"It was definitely murder then, and not something else, robbery or accident?"

77

"It appears to be murder, yes."

Captain Sweetman went to leave. Mary followed.

"Anything more you'd like to add, Captain?"

"I wish I knew more, Ms. Bartlett. That's it for now. Sergeant, Charley's crew is going to be here for another hour probably. See that no one enters the crime area until they leave. Good day Ms. Bartlett."

Mary watched the Captain get into his brown Dodge Reliant. His tailored look seemed more appropriate for a Rolls Royce.

"Snappy dresser, your boss," said Mary.

"Public relations. Now you heard the Captain, stay away from the crime area."

"Is the boathouse part of the crime area? I have to make a phone call."

"Fine with me, if Dace doesn't care."

"Thanks, Sarge, for all your help."

"Anytime, *Ms*. Bartlett."

Reaching the top of the stairs, Mary could see Dutch staring out over the river, his back slightly stooped and, from this angle, cigarette smoke curling out of the top of his head. Mary had always thought Dutch put up with her because she was one of the few people who didn't chastise him for smoking. Quite the contrary. Mary thought of Dutch Dace as incomplete without that Camel. The man had the lean nonchalance and leathery look of another time, a time when sports figures endorsed smoking, when pilots wore white scarves and soldiers about to die were given a last puff, at least in the movies. Winston Wyc should meet Dutch Dace. If the man was really an historian then Dutch would be somebody he'd like to know, for Dutch knew more about the history of The Hudson River than any person dead or alive. The problem was getting him to talk about what he knew to strangers. Mary had a feeling though that the two men would like each other. Wyc seemed to be a person who wasn't afraid of silences as part of the conversation. Of course she could be wrong. It did happen.

"River throwing up some strange fish, I hear."

Mary leaned on the railing next to Dutch.

"What took you so long? The man's been dead for almost three hours."

Dutch didn't look at Mary but continued to study the water. She studied his profile, his wry smile.

"Been up at the fort pissing off Conran."

Flicking his cigarette out into the water, Dutch turned to face Mary.

"I'm going to have a drink. Join me?"

"Love to. Where'd it happen?"

"About fifty yards down past the dock. Jack D?"

"What else. Some ice this time. See who did it?"

Hesitating, Dutch held the screen door open for a moment, his head tilted upward. He spoke without turning.

"Maybe you ask too many questions."

"It's true. I'm a nosy bitch."

Mary flinched as Dutch let the screen door bang shut behind him.

Chapter 8

The section of the castle where Winston was being bedded looked like a medieval SRO for transients. A windowless stone cell held little more than a cot, a dry sink and a few hooks for hanging your clothes—or yourself, thought Winston. You'd have to be truly despondent to spend good money for the privilege to sleep here. Winston peered behind the door for the chamber pot.

"I know it seems grim at first glance, Winston, but our deliverees are not here for the creature comforts. They come to rest, to look inward and rediscover . . . that whatever-it-was they now feel is missing in their lives. The silence here is wonderful."

"I can imagine. How thick are these walls?"

"Eighteen inches." Conran gave the stones nearest him a good whack with his open palm. "One can be completely alone, cut off from people, from light, from sound . . . everything. If one chooses."

Wonderful, thought Winston. When the killer comes for me nobody will hear the screams.

"Didn't the Count of Monte Cristo stay here?" The Ramada Inn was starting to look good. And cheap.

Conran chuckled. "Very good, Winston. It does

have a certain look, I agree, but we don't lock the doors. One is free to come and go as one wishes. As you are aware the grounds are quite opulent. This is to balance off the austerity of the sleeping quarters which the deliverees can use solely to concentrate on important, inner matters. If they want to be stroked they can spend their time at a spa. The retreat is concerned with one's spiritual health."

Winston could see that Conran took it all very seriously. Connecting with the inner person was obviously important to him and to his guests. Winston on the other hand had always been afraid of what might lurk beneath his subconscious and studiously stayed away. Normally his outer person was too much for him; heaven forbid he should awaken the slumbering monster of his id or whatever it was called that frolicked under his ego.

"And bathroom facilities . . . ?"

"Just down the hall on the left and you'll be glad to know that the baths are wonderfully modern. Seems no matter how ready people are willing to chastise themselves, when it comes to the bath, they want comfort."

Sounded reasonable to Winston.

"There's a small closet on the left as you enter the bath. I think you'll find everything you need for the night in there."

Conran stood proudly. Go ahead, he seemed to say. Find fault, you non-believer. Run your white glove above the door casing. Check for dust motes under the cot. Inspect not only our brand of toothpaste but our sincerity. We run a tight ship here and don't mind the bodies.

"Thank you. I don't mean to be an inconvenience."

"Don't be silly."

"Look . . . I know we mentioned a tour but could I

just get a few things from my car and rest a bit? I'm still a little wobbly from recent events.''

"Oh . . . of course. I must admit I feel slightly . . . what's the word, slightly disconnected myself. As if it never really happened.'' Conran checked out the middle distance. "The whole horrible thing is going to hit me at some point, I know, and then . . .'' Conran could only shake his head at the confusion to come.

Winston said nothing. He wanted to be alone and didn't know how to say it gracefully. A sudden breakdown by Conran was not something he wanted to witness. And why was Conran scared to be left by himself? Did he know something Winston should know?

"Well . . . I eh, guess I'll leave you to settle in. If there's anything you might need: information, more blankets, some small talk . . .'' Conran shrugged. ". . . just come down to the reception office and whoever's there can certainly get in touch with me. Anything.''

"Thanks.''

"Oh. Dinner's at seven-thirty. In the main dining room. It's off the entrance hall, kitty-corner to the library, you can't miss it. The dining room is quite baronial. You'll love it. Do join us. It'll be only a few staff and us.''

Seven-thirty sounded a little early for Winston's blood, but since his presence wasn't being demanded, why not give the impression of coming and then not show. He could always claim he got lost.

"Thanks again. Sounds like fun.''

"Simple fare but healthy. We don't encourage the eating of meat here.''

Punctuating his leaving with a few nods and a deep sigh, Conran finally shut the door behind him.

Winston stood in his cell waiting for the key to turn. The bolt to slide. Healthy. That's all he had to hear. Not only had he been thrown into the dungeon but they were threatening to force brown rice and bean curd under his fingernails. He'd tell them anything they wanted to know. Except who did it. That he couldn't tell them. Maybe it *had* been Conran who did in Mr. Barefoot. What if Conran thought that Winston had seen him? But that was impossible. Someone else had moved just beyond that curtain of vegetation and it wasn't Conran or Barefoot.

Sitting on his cot, Winston once again went over the past three hours. The conclusion was always the same: he had no idea who it could be. None of the people he had met seemed capable of murder. He was sure, other than Conran, the rest had remained in the castle. Maybe the albatross? Winston would check with Miss Pinklingill to see if Mary Crosse had abandoned her at any time during the library break. The Engine had certainly seemed in a big hurry when Winston spotted them from the window. And then there was that Dace fellow. He looked like a man who had been there and back so many times, it now came to him. And what was it he had said?

Winston moved about the room inspecting the stones for cracks or holes where hidden viewing devices might be secreted. This comes from reading too many thrillers he thought, admonishing himself for his paranoia. Maybe a long sit on my cot would be nice. Meditate a little. Throw caution to the wind, peel back a few layers, find that child hidden among the neurons. How about the adult? Shaking his head, Winston decided to forsake an exploration of himself and continue a solo exploration of the castle. This Smelton character was definitely something of a romantic. The castle was probably rife with secret nooks and crannies, hallways that led nowhere, rooms reached by knowing which stone to push. Remembering seeing a staircase at the end of the hall, Winston, peeking first this way then that, shut his door behind him and headed for the stairs.

There were eight other rooms between Winston's and the end of the hall, but all the doors were closed and he couldn't tell if any of them were occupied. One was labeled with a small porcelain plaque that read Bath. As he ascended the stairs, Winston made a mental note to ask Conran if these rooms had been added after the Oblates purchased the castle or, if not, what in the world had possessed Smelton to build them. Could the man have had his own private prison system for out-of-hand weekend guests?

The staircase was of stone and spiraled up to one of the belvederes that Winston had spied on his arrival. A fifteen by fifteen foot enclosed deck commanded a breathtaking view of the grounds and the Hudson River. From here Smelton would have seen the steamboat full of house guests long before they disembarked. Winston could see the boathouse and down the river for about a mile. On the opposite shore the Hudson-Harlem railroad tracks were visible, then a steep embankment and houses among the greenery. North of there would be New Holland and twenty miles east, the village of Wistfield. Winston had discovered his first dead person in that small hamlet, an experience that had initially darkened his thoughts concerning the bucolic. However, there had been an incredible young lady too, and for a time after that trauma Winston had been a constant weekend visitor. But living in two different worlds had proven too big a strain, and as the trips back and forth became farther apart, the love of the century had fizzled and failed. Unhappily for Winston, the incredible lady wouldn't give up family, the good life, and a thriving business to join him in poverty in New York City. He still didn't get it. Amazing, but that was only a year and a half ago. Maybe a little side trip . . . nahhhh.

Against the south railing of the deck stood a secured set of binoculars, a simplified version of the kind one sees on ocean boardwalks. Happy to see that the Oblates hadn't installed a coin slot, Winston bent down to peer through the lens. It took him a moment to realize that the wavy lines he was looking at was the river. Turning a few dials he brought the river and then the riverbank into focus. Tilting the binoculars to the left, he could see the boathouse. Standing there in the circle of the lens stood Mr. Dace and that reporter Mary Bartlett, glasses raised in what appeared to be a salute. Winston straightened up. What in the world were those two celebrating? And what was she doing there? Hearing a sound behind him, Winston was surprised to find an elderly gentleman grinning at him from the stairwell opening.

"My . . . well, I wasn't expecting anyone and . . ." The man hovered in the doorway like a marionette.

"I'm sorry, I was just wandering around and . . . the view here is wonderful." Indicating with his hand the vista over his left shoulder, Winston grimaced at the use of the word "wonderful." He hated that word and felt it fell in line right behind "interesting."

"It's my favorite. Always has been." The gentleman took a hesitant step onto the belvedere deck. Pleasantly thin, the man was dressed in a rough, silk shirt tucked into what appeared to be tuxedo trousers. With two puffs of white hair over each ear and a slightly larger puff sitting upon his head, the man looked like a geriatric Bozo the Clown.

"You come up here a lot?" asked Winston.

"I've been up here twice today already. There was quite a commotion earlier down at the boathouse. I was looking through the glasses."

"What did you see?"

"See? Well . . . it's time to move on. Maybe I'm hungry. My, my . . . well, so long." The man took one more quick look at Winston over his shoulder and disappeared back down the stairs.

"Wait . . ." Winston hurried after the man but he was gone. The stairwell was empty. That's odd, thought Winston, he couldn't have gotten down these stairs that fast, or could he? And no sound of footsteps in the hall. Winston descended a few steps, stopped and listened. The spiral stairs were silent. The whole castle was silent, not a single sound other than Winston's breathing. Suddenly he felt spooked, the small hairs at the back of his neck danced. Standing in the half-light coming from the belvedere, Winston decided that he didn't want to spend the night at Smelton Castle. For all he knew the satyrs leapt from the chimney surrounds at midnight and went about molesting guests. The idea of sitting in his cold, stone cell after a spirited meal of tofu and bean sprouts was more than he could imagine. Not ten minutes ago he had seen Mary Bartlett raising a suspicious glass down at the boathouse. Winston knew what he had to do.

Chapter 9

Parking behind the boathouse, Winston took a moment to reconcile himself to the surroundings. Nearly four hours before, the area had been busy with police and the machinery necessary to examine violent death. He remembered an emergency vehicle had left its revolving light on and how it had lit the side of Captain Sweetman's face. Dark then light, dark then light, until Winston had had to move away. Thinking back, he couldn't recall any sound, only movement. Silent vignettes played out in the strobe of the ambulance light against the backdrop of the river and the distant sailboats. Most of the policemen and many of the emergency crews had stood around wondering what to do, looking officious and disconcerted, eyeing the bushes for hidden killers. Only those few with specific jobs moved with any purpose. One man and an assistant dusted trees and rocks for fingerprints. Another three men appeared specialists in the search for clues. Sweetman had told everyone else not to come near the spot where the body had been found. A yellow ribbon had been attached to various trees corralling the "spot," delineating the off-limits area. Winston had been given a ride back up to the castle by a young officer as shaken as he was by the event. Barefoot had still lain on the riverbank, a man dozing in the late afternoon sun.

All was quiet at the moment. The sun had made its journey across the river and was now behind Winston, its late afternoon rays pushing the shadow of the boathouse well out into the water. Coming to the stairs that led up to the boathouse deck, Winston could hear Mary laughing. "Hello," he called. Dace's face peered at him through an embrasure in the battlements.

"It's the historian," said Mary, leaning over next to Dace. "Returned to the scene of the crime. Come on up."

"Hope I'm not disturbing anything," said Winston as he ducked under Dace's clothesline and stood in the middle of the deck, feeling very much as if he was. Mary and Dace faced him from the crenelated parapet that ran around the open space. Quarry tile added to the feudal look of the deck which served for Dace as an outdoor laundry, dining room and summer living area. An old washing machine, the type with hand cranked rollers for rinsing and drying, stood over to one side. Winston recognized it as the same kind his mother had used for years in their basement. Mom had said it was from the Middle Ages. Fortunately for young Winston and his friends, it had never been removed after his mother had finally gotten her new Maytag. The rollers had proved perfect for eliminating the unending supply of spiders and centipedes that thrived in the dark recesses of his basement. The end had come when Mom had found a garter snake dangling from between the rollers, one half still round and firm, the other half flat as a newly rinsed T-shirt.

In the center of the deck was a redwood picnic table covered with a blue and white checked oil cloth. Near the parapet by the river sat two old, corduroy armchairs worn smooth by occupancy and weather. Winston was surprised to see all the furniture. He hadn't noticed it the first time around.

"Not at all. In fact, I was just talking about you," answered Mary.

"That the reason I heard you laughing?"

"Not really. Dutch here said something funny about historians."

Winston waited for the joke but it wasn't offered.

"Dutch and I were wondering what the monastery wanted with you, Mr. Wyc." Screwing up her eyes Mary regarded Winston with suspicion. "You know, your name rings a bell for some reason. I can't figure it out though. You ever spend time in New Holland?"

"Not long enough to leave a trail."

"It'll come to me. You doing research on castles?"

"I'm here at the request of Mr. Conran," said Winston wondering how much information he was allowed to confer.

"And . . . ?" Mary affected an attentive leer. "What's the big deal? He hire you to bump off Barefoot?" She gave Dace a wry smile.

"That was it." Winston wondered if Mary ever gave up the reporter's harangue. "Sunsets must be pretty good from here." He addressed Dace.

"More colors than an oil slick, Cap." Dutch had moved farther down the deck.

"Why don't you offer your guest a drink, Dutch? I bet he could use one."

Dutch thought about the request.

"Jack Daniel's all right?"

"I'd love one. I've a thirst a parish priest would

89

sell his soul for."

Dutch smiled, a thin line that cut across the lower half of his face and crinkled the eyes. Dutch stopped beside Winston on his way to the screen door. "Don't mind her. She's always a pain in the ass."

"It's true." Mary's face was working up to one of her big smiles, the eyes radiating mischief. "You haven't answered my question."

"Contract killing is only a sideline of mine, to make ends meet. Historians are at the low end of the money ladder."

Mary completed the smile and her whole face shone, warm and guileless. Immediately Winston's guard went up.

"Now why are you here? I promise it's my last question."

Winston sat at the picnic table. "Conran wants to have the estate placed on the Registry of Historic Places in Washington."

"Really? Does this place have any historic significance?"

Winston shrugged. He probably had already said too much. Dace came back through the screen door, two drinks in hand.

"What's the story, Dutch? This pile of rocks worth anything in the history books?"

Dace shook his head in the negative. "Thought that was your last question."

"You gonna do it?" asked Mary turning back to Winston and ignoring Dace's remark.

"It's a long process. I just do the paper work. Washington has the final word. I'd like it if we could leave this info out of the paper."

"Well . . . I can do that." Mary sat down next to Winston. "See, I'm not so bad. Was Justin Barefoot all for getting an historical plaque hung on the castle wall?"

"I . . . I don't know."

Winston could see the headline now: Board Member Whacked for Plaque.

"Yeah you do but you're not telling. That's okay. Look, I'm not the bad guy here, someone else has that honor. I'm only looking for a motive. I know I'm being a little offensive but I am a reporter and this whole thing is exciting. We don't have many murders in New Holland."

"A little?"

"Okay, a lot. You like me though, I can tell. What do you think of my hair? Too short?"

Winston smiled. "It does wonders for your cheekbones."

Mary put her head back and laughed. Sliding off the table, she crossed the deck to Dutch.

"See. Not everyone is of your opinion."

"What have I ever said?" Dace smiled over at Winston who smiled back. This was not the same man who called the police earlier. That man had been guarded and taciturn, almost scary. Not the type to let strangers walk into his life. Initially Winston had thought Dace might be the killer. Now he didn't know.

"You didn't have to say anything, I could tell. Can I use the phone? I want to blow Bossman off his pedestal." Mary turned to Winston. "That's my editor in chief. I'm about to become his star reporter."

Frowning, Dace looked in the direction of the screen door.

"I knew you wouldn't mind," said Mary hoisting her bag, and heading for the door, letting it slam behind her. Dace shook his head. Moving over to the parapet, he stood in profile to Winston.

"Just like Mary not to introduce us. My friends call me Dutch."

"Nice to finally meet you. I'm Winston."

"Mary has a better feel for people than I do. Part of her job, I guess. She thinks you're okay."

Dutch's voice implied he was reserving judgment. The two men looked in silence out at the river. Inside, Mary could be heard rattling off indistinct words to someone at the *New Holland Observer*.

"Not a bad view," said Winston.

The Hudson lay wide and flat and close at this point, more a large lake or a harbor than a river. The far bank glistened with reflective sunlight. Being so near, Winston could hear the vast water's moving, a murmuring like the quiet strumming of a magnificent cello, a resonant underscoring to all the other sounds around them.

"You're lucky to live so close to the Hudson."

"Wouldn't know. I've never lived very far from its banks."

Dutch sounds like a wealthy man who's never known poverty, thought Winston. What could all those poor people be complaining about? Getting up from the table, he moved over to the parapet near Dutch. Below him the large boat rocked gently against the dock. It seemed impressive to Winston although the extent of his nautical experience was rowing around Central Park Lake in a small dinghy.

"Nice boat," Winston said lamely.

"You know about boats?"

Some of the light reappeared in Dutch's hooded eyes.

"Well . . . no, not a thing really. In fact, I've never been on one longer than a few feet."

Dutch gave him a look bordering on pity.

"This is a special rig put together by Lyman Morse up in Maine. It's a modification of a trawler."

Moving closer, Dutch took his time lighting a Camel and then, bending at the waist, rested his long forearms on the concrete parapet.

"A trawler? You mean a commercial fishing boat?" asked Winston.

"That's right. Tough thing to do, modify an existing design. Any time you add or take away from what's already there you can run into problems. This boat had a deep-V hull which made the adaptation possible."

Winston nodded, having no idea what Dutch was talking about.

"The guys up in Maine added five feet to the stern of the original rig, moved the galley forward, and stuck a large, aluminum fuel tank under the double berth in the stern. There's no keel or skeg, which adds a few knots for speed."

"Get the guests back and forth from New York quickly, huh?"

"Something like that." Dutch flicked his cigarette into the water. "Mary might be a while. Want to see the boat?"

"Sure."

Following Dutch down the stairs and onto the dock, Winston could hear Mary through an open window talking quickly and excitedly. The words "historian" and "Conran" came to him and suddenly Winston wished he'd never said a thing to this overzealous, undercoiffed Mary Bartlett. The monastery was not going to be thrilled if she overplayed the small amount of detail he had given her.

The boat rolled gently under them as they stepped onto the deck. Winston had wandered marinas before and he was always amazed at how shiny the decks of pleasure boats appeared. Like fire engines, they seemed to get a lot of attention in the polishing area.

"Strange name for a boat. The *Hyorky?* Something to do with the castle?"

"Not this castle, Cap."

"I see." Dutch for some reason didn't seem to want to talk about it. Maybe Winston should stick to numbers. "How long is the boat?"

"Fifty-two feet. Beam is fifteen foot, give or take a few inches. It's built to be comfortable inside."

Winston followed Dutch around to the rear of the boat.

"The aft deck area easily seats ten. You enter the salon through that hatchway." Down three steps through a low door Winston followed Dutch into a large living area.

"Bedroom's through there. Galley that way. There's a bath in both spaces. Salon here's about the only part really used. Rarely is the boat needed for overnight."

Dutch sounded like a man who'd been through the spiel too many times. Every guest that showed up at the monastery probably wanted the tour if not the ride back and forth from New York. And Dutch was right, this boat was certainly built for comfort. A banquette and three club chairs were all upholstered in soft, tan colored leather. Highly polished, mahogany cabinet doors hid an entertainment center, a small library and a bar. Winston admired boat designers for their ability to cram so much into so little a space and have it all look right. These people should design the interiors of the new apartments being constructed in the City where the rooms keep getting smaller. Of course it helps to have a large body of water just outside your door. Even so, this boat sitting on a rooftop of a twenty story co-op would fetch a nice price.

"So what's an architectural historian do?" Dutch settled against the arm of the banquette built into the hatchway wall.

"Some write books on the history of buildings, cities, that sort of thing. Others try to explain different cultures through their architecture. They're academics, mostly."

"Sounds boring."

"Can be I guess. I'm one of the few who treats the field as a business. I do general historical research for individuals or corporations. Someone needs to locate original architectural and structural drawings for use in renovation or restoration, they call me. I've even searched for evidentiary material for use in legal cases. But the rent is paid by my representing clients before local and national historic agencies."

"Like monasteries."

"Whatever comes along."

"Still sounds boring."

Winston couldn't argue. "Well it certainly isn't the same as driving around on a yacht for a living," he said, looking into the galley. He turned around to find Dutch smiling at him. The long, leathery face wrinkled with amusement.

"Come on, I'll show you where we . . . drive this rig."

Dutch let Winston go before him into the pilot-house. Winston gave out a low whistle as he examined the instrument panel.

"Does NASA know about this? You'd need a degree in nautical space flight to pilot this ship," Winston marveled. "Why so complicated?"

"It's not that bad. This is mostly radio and radar. You start carrying passengers and the government wants certain safety features. These instruments monitor the twin 680 horsepower diesel engines that sit below the galley."

"Sounds like a lot of power."

Running his hand over the panel, Dutch smiled his wire-like smile.

"It's okay."

Turning, Winston looked back down the river to where Barefoot's body had been found. A string of yellow ribbon could be seen.

"Did you know Mr. Barefoot very well?" asked Winston staring at the spot.

"I'd talk with him sometimes. He didn't fraternize too much, if that's the right word."

Winston could understand that having met the man. Justin Barefoot probably kept a safe distance between himself and the help.

"Why would anyone want to kill him?"

Dutch shrugged. "Who knows why people kill each other? Maybe to keep them from rocking the boat."

As it were, thought Winston, wondering if Dutch was being ironic. He didn't seem the type. Watching Dutch move about the pilothouse, Winston suddenly remembered their first conversation on the boat-house deck. When Winston had reported finding the body, Dutch had said "already?" What could that have meant? Was Dutch referring to Barefoot or to something else? Again the sinewy Mr. Dace wasn't looking so trustworthy. Winston made a mental note to tell Captain Sweetman of the conversation as Mary came out of the boathouse and down the stairs. She talked up to them from the dock.

"I have to get back to the paper. Bossman is jumping up and down."

"I can't wait to read the morning paper," said Winston.

"Don't sound so apprehensive. The first report deals mainly with the facts. As the rest of the media tries to catch up we get into the human interest end. That's you."

"I don't consider myself a very interesting human."

Mary jumped onto the boat.

"You don't? Talking to Bossman I suddenly remembered where I'd heard the name Wyc. You were involved in the Good Luck murders from a couple years back. Am I not right?" Mary gave Dutch her "I got him" look. Dutch was impressed. Raising his eyebrows, his expression was one of positive reappraisal.

"You *had* to remember," Winston grumbled.

"Don't look so glum. If I recall properly you had a lot to do with the solving of that case."

"Hardly. I managed to always be in the wrong place at the wrong time. Nearly got me killed."

"I tried to interview you. Never got past your land-lady." Excitedly pacing the pilothouse, Mary's face fixed on Winston's.

"What are you thinking?" asked Winston, sitting. Mary sat beside him.

"Well pal, I'm afraid you're in the wrong place at the wrong time again, but this time you have help."

"What does that mean?" But Winston already knew.

"I think together we can solve this thing. What do you think, Dutch?" Mary was again on her feet. "Wyc, you're the star witness, the one who was in the castle before the murder, nearly *saw* the murder. I know the background here, the history. Dutch knows the staff. What do you say?"

Dutch looked dubious. Winston was appalled.

"Forget it. I'm not in the murder solving racket. I'm a low-life architectural historian out on his lonesome trying to turn a buck and not at all interested in pissing off some homicidal maniac. I've many good years before me."

"Oh come on, Winston. This is your chance to be a hero."

"Hero? It's my chance to assist a young reporter trying to advance her career. No thanks."

"Look I've got to go. There's a deadline to meet, but I want to see you later. Promise?"

"I promise nothing."

"We'll have something to eat and a nice interview and you can explain about saving history or whatever it is you do, and I can try to convince you to stick around a few days."

"Dinner would be nice but I'm supposed to have dinner with Mr. Conran up at the monastery."

"You're kidding. All they serve is baked tofu and sticky, brown rice . . . *with* the husks still on. Ugh."

Winston had been afraid of that. Mary grasped his arm.

"I gave you my card, call me. We can meet later. It's almost seven now, how about calling me around . . . around ten thirty. I should be back by then. I only live a short distance down the river from here. You could almost walk."

"I'll call but I promise nothing."

Mary beamed at him. "I've got to go. Thanks for the drink, Dutch. Talk to you later."

Winston could feel the boat rock as Mary jumped onto the deck. Dutch didn't look all that happy. The darkness had returned to his eyes.

"I better go, too," said Winston. "I'm supposed to

be at the dining hall by seven-thirty. Thanks for the tour."

"No problem, Cap. I think you'd be nuts to chase after this killer with Mary. Could be dangerous."

"Don't worry, I've no intention of helping her and when I see her later it'll be to talk her out of pursuing it."

Dutch nodded in agreement.

Outside, Winston wondered for a moment if Mary and Dutch could be related. They had the height and the same high, round cheekbones. Also they seemed to enjoy that bond that only family can have, an affinity, an affectionate disrespect that related gene pools can have for one another. Was blood thicker than river water? Had Dutch been the one to tip off Mary to Barefoot's murder? He hadn't acted completely surprised when Winston had knocked on his door. Winston would do some snooping himself before his meeting later with Mary. Conran seemed the type to enjoy a little gossiping. The inside tale on Dutch might be the only thing to save dinner. That and watching the sunset afterward from the belvedere over his room.

Chapter 10

Standing in the hall outside the dining room, Winston let his mind wander back up the stairs and past the little sign that read Private. If his calculations were correct, the dining area would be the large room he'd spied through the peepholes earlier in the day. Maybe he could sneak up and see what was being served.

"Psssst."

Stiffening, Winston cautioned a look in the direction of the hiss.

"Winston," a voice said. "Over here."

"Who's there?" Winston squinted into the dimness of the darkening conservatory.

"It's me." The round face of Eric Shrove leaned out and then back into shadow. "We have to talk."

"Can't we talk out here in the hall? Since this afternoon I've sworn off dark, shadowy places."

"I need to talk to you in private."

"How about outside on the portico? Or on the lawn."

"Someone might see me with you."

Winston moved a few steps toward the hushed voice and stopped.

"This is as close as I come. And I'd appreciate your coming out of the dark. I don't like talking to a phantom."

Eric moved timidly out of the shadows, his eyes darting about the hall and up the stairs. The man not only sounded like a ghost, he looked like one.

"You okay?" asked Winston.

"I think so. That shot they gave me really did me in. I must apologize. I'm afraid I acted somewhat the fool back in the library . . . it's just that the . . . news was such a shock."

"No need to apologize. Mr. Barefoot was a close friend of yours and . . ."

"But he wasn't really. I mean we knew each other but we weren't what you'd call friends. I admired Justin. I mean he knew so much about art and things and was . . . well, he was from another world." Eric thought about that for a moment. "We never saw one another actually unless it had to do with the retreat. Listen." Looking cautiously around the hall, Eric took Winston by the arm. "You're the only person here that I can trust. I think my own life may be in danger."

"Why's that?" Looking around, Winston wasn't sure he wanted to know. Eric assumed his "chubby little boy caught in the cookie jar" pose: hands clasped in front, chin on chest.

"I can't tell you why but if something happens to me tonight, I've left a . . ."

"Eric! Good to see you up and about. How are we feeling?"

Michael Conran came bustling through the portico doors and into the fading light of the hallway. Veering to his left, he went to the wall and switched on the lights, two wrought iron chandeliers hanging far above them. Eric's eyes grew round with . . . with

101

what? Fright or surprise, Winston couldn't tell; the light from above threw odd shadows on all their faces. Eric clutched his arm in a tight fist before letting go to face Conran.

"I'm not very brave when it comes to *that* kind of shock, I'm afraid. I'm okay now, thank you."

"Well, good." Conran gave Eric a big hug. "Come to join us for a meal, I see. Best thing for you, a healthy, nutritional meal."

"A meal . . . ? I'm not . . ." Eric squirmed in Conran's hearty clasp.

"And you too, Winston. Good to see you here. We'll have a fine dinner. Lots of talk about the importance of castles, hey."

Conran had changed into a dark green cowl for dinner, a garment that instead of falling to his ankles stopped at his waist, having pants made of the same heavy cotton material. The hood fell open down his back. His feet were shod in the requisite sandals, his toes having a well manicured look.

"Will Cynthia be joining us?" asked Winston heading for the double doors. It was time to rescue Eric who'd just received another bone-crushing squeeze and was beginning to look like a balloon losing air.

"It's up in the air, Winston. She may join us for coffee. You seem to have a soft spot for our Ms.Shea."

"She seems bright and sensible, qualities I like."

"And she's attractive . . ."

"I'd be lying if I said I hadn't noticed."

Conran nodded his head in approval. Moving past Winston, he threw open the doors to the dining room.

Conran had described the dining room as baronial and he had been almost correct. The room wasn't Gallic but Norse, looking more like the grand mead hall of Asgard than the banquet hall of Camelot. No knight ever relaxed in a hall resembling this one. Rough board walls held leather shields and broad axes, formidable looking clubs of all sorts, furred helmets with horns, and over the walk-in fireplace at the far end, a ten foot model of a Viking longboat. The irregular, bluestone floor, polished to a fare-thee-well, reflected the uneven light from the candle sconces that lined the walls. The room was forty feet wide, seventy feet long and three stories high. Sunlight from two huge skylights barely reached the floor. Narrow windows with wavy, handblown glass looked to the outside. Confused at first as to how the room could look out on all sides, Winston, on closer inspection, realized that the windows were merely for effect. The woodland scenes were trompe l'oeil.

"Very effective, wouldn't you say?"

Conran spoke over Winston's right shoulder.

"The scenes are painted to match the outside," observed Winston.

"That's right, not everyone notices. Isn't it wonderful, Winston? The Hudson glides along below forever in summer."

"It's different."

"I knew you'd like it. The dining room began as a smaller affair but one of the Smeltons, the third one I believe, went gaga over anything Scandinavian. I think *Beowulf* changed his life. Anyway he redid the original banquet room by making it larger, removing a floor above it and adding the windows. Plus all the paraphernalia, of course. He started a Norse society that met here for two weeks every year, everyone pretending to be some member of the Aesir. They would wear hides, helmets with antlers, whack each other with swords, that sort of thing. Rather silly if you ask me."

103

Winston wondered if any of the members dressed up like druids or monks . . . or robin's eggs.

"Did the Vikings have a religion?" asked Winston.

"What?"

"Nothing. Where shall we sit?"

"Over here would be nice. The last rays of the sun hit that far wall. One of the Smeltons put a reflector up on the roof to catch the setting sunlight and bounce it down here. On a clear evening it can be quite striking."

Twenty long tables made of rough wood were arranged in boarding school fashion, two abreast and lined up one behind the other, each capable of seating from ten to fourteen people. The weekends must be busy. Three kitchen helpers dressed in whites sat at a table near the kitchen entrance, their convivial manner subsiding considerably as Conran entered.

Upon sitting, Winston studied the opposite wall for the presence of peepholes but none could be detected in the coarse and grainy patterns of the rough wood. Winston felt uncomfortable knowing that someone could be watching him and made a mental note to observe acceptable table manners. Conran disappeared into the kitchen.

"I might excuse myself," said Eric leaning in toward Winston. "Justin told me the food here is disgusting, a form of punishment for living well. Maybe you could tell Michael I didn't feel so good."

"Wait a minute. What was it you started to tell me out in the hall. You were going to leave something . . ."

"Oh."

If Winston hadn't known about the peepholes, Eric's quick inspection of the opposite wall would have meant nothing, but he did, and he realized that Eric was afraid of saying anything that might place him in jeopardy. In fact, he ignored Winston's question.

"Actually, I *don't* feel very well." Eric began to rise as Conran came bustling back into the dining room.

"Good news. Chef Carol has come up with something I think you're going to like very much. She wasn't expecting to feed anyone but staff, seems I forgot to inform the kitchen of our extra guests . . . but she is happy to oblige." Bending down in a conspiratorial manner, Conran lowered his voice. "You know how temperamental these cooks can be."

Making a pinched face, Eric exchanged a quick glance with Winston.

"You know Michael, I was just saying to Winston here that I didn't actually . . ."

Eric's bid for freedom was cut off by the sudden banging open of the double doors and the entrance of Miss Pinkingill and her attendant engine. Stopping to take in the situation, Miss Pinkingill gave the room a thorough going-over before mumbling something to Sister Mary Crosse who then went into overdrive, reaching their table in a sprint. Melody Pinklingill didn't seem to mind the abrupt thrust, the rush and the sudden stop which tossed her thin body forward. Winston was surprised Sister Mary didn't leave little tire burns on the castle floors.

"What a pleasant surprise, Melody. Welcome." Obviously taken aback, Conran gave a brief nod in the Engine's direction.

"Why thank you, Michael. Events being what they were today that old house of mine suddenly felt too big, too empty. I hope you don't mind if Mary and I seek a little comfort in your company."

Melody straightened her dress.

"Good gracious, no. Please be seated. It's . . . it's almost a party."

"Hmmmm." Melody made a wry face.

"Look . . . I . . . eh. . . ." A little color drained from Conran's face as he stared over at the kitchen door. "Of course, I must talk to Chef Carol . . ."

Winston noticed Conran hesitate before entering the kitchen. The seated staff members had disappeared.

"A party, huh?" Melody motioned for Sister Mary to maneuver her into the table. "I would have thought the mood here somewhat more somber what with the . . . passing of an old friend." She sucked at her cheeks making her thin face even thinner. "You feeling festive, Mr. Shrove?"

"No, I'm not. In fact just the opposite."

"And Mr. Wyc? I see you haven't flown the coop."

"Not yet. Captain Sweetman seems to think I can help him in some way with his investigation."

"Is that true? Can you help?"

"I really don't see how. I've told him everything I know."

Melody Pinklingill had introduced a whole new tension into the situation and Winston wanted a drink. His blood sugar was plummeting.

"I see. Well, I for one am glad to have you here this evening. I want to hear more about this saving our dear property from the clutches of evil."

Sister Mary squeaked out a titter. Melody turned to look at her.

"Quit making silly noises and sit down, Mary. How long since we've been in this dining room?"

"Two years, September."

"That long. My, my."

"Food that good," said Winston wryly.

"Let's say good *for* you, Mr. Wyc. I'm not a big eater, myself. All I ask is that the food be fresh, whatever it is. Grew up that way, I guess, and it hasn't killed me yet."

Winston had grown up in a meat and potatoes house. His mother had been a firm believer in "food well cooked was food without harm." His father was a butcher and had brought home beautiful cuts of meat which mother then cooked down into hard, gray little balls surrounded by puddles of color, an abstractionist's idea of vegetables. Once, when Winston was ten, he and his father had gone out for a Sunday dinner. How his father had swung that, he couldn't recall, but they went to a restaurant in the neighborhood, Lou's Steak House, which he learned later was famous for its meat. The meal had been an initiation of sorts into the cuisine beyond his own kitchen. Winston's father had stared at his plate for a full half minute before speaking, his face aglow with anticipation.

"See this bean, son, and this potato. And this piece of meat. Notice how the flesh of this steak bounces back when flattened with a fork, the dark juices. And when sliced, the pink color fading into a darker red near the middle. The knife glides through the meat like it was butter. Try it."

His father had waited, leaning into the table as Winston had stared into his own plate at the red-wet, and, for him, uncooked beef. Winston had gagged. Not a word had been said and Winston had still been able to have dessert even though his plate had been barely touched. Later, much later, Winston realized that his father hadn't expected him to eat the food that day; the fact that Winston had been introduced to properly prepared food had been enough. At least his son would not be surprised when it showed up again.

Winston's remembrance was interrupted by raised voices from the kitchen.

"Seems Chef Carol wasn't prepared for this many people," smiled Eric.

"What if she refuses to cook anything? Could we be in for another murder?" quipped Winston.

"No more murders, please." Placing a small pocket watch on the table, Miss Pinklingill snapped it open. "You find your accommodations adequate, Mr. Wyc?"

"Adequate is the right word."

"I take it Micahel has put you up in one of his contemplative cells."

"He has. Actually I've asked him to remove the cot and the blankets from the room. I'm going to go all the way and sleep on the floor. Naked." Winston's remark was met with looks of concern. He smiled over at Sister Crosse. "Only kidding, folks."

"Very droll, Mr. Wyc," said Miss Pinklingill, forcing a smile. "I take it you don't necessarily see the . . . the importance of Michael's work here."

"I'm sorry, I didn't mean to belittle it. Having been raised in the all encompassing arms of the Catholic church I tend to let those with an inside track worry about my spiritual shortcomings. It frees me to be glib."

"I see . . . well, that rather supports my first impressions. If you don't mind my saying, you did not strike me as the contemplative sort, Mr. Wyc. Believing that, I worried that you might be put off by the spartan quality of the surroundings. Therefore I was going to offer you a room at my house. A comfortable room."

Touché, thought Winston. Better watch my belittlements.

"How nice of you to offer but I thought Eric was staying at your house tonight."

"What?" Eric was surprised.

"It had been discussed..." Miss Pinklingill leaned over to address Eric. "...while you were resting. Nothing confirmed, mind you. You are certainly welcome."

"I..."

Conran came back through the kitchen door, his face a forced mask of cheerfulness. Sitting, he glanced back at the kitchen before speaking in a low monotone.

"Chef Carol is a saint."

Eric interrupted the long quiet that followed.

"Actually Michael, I was thinking that I might..."

"We are to have a wonderful meal." Almost shouting, Conran suddenly shook himself from his disgruntled state. His body straightening, his face once again lively, the grand crinkles and dimples coming to life, ready to feed and entertain.

"A splendid meal, indeed."

Conran's exuberance was met with looks of distress.

"There's been a... death, Michael," said Miss Pinklingill.

"Of course there has been and I as much as anyone else have been greatly disturbed by what has happened here today. But walking hand in hand with my sadness is the joy of knowing that Justin has gone to a better world; a world of peace and everlasting comfort. It is this knowing that allows me to go on living. Brooding does no one any good."

Bad for the digestion too, thought Winston.

"I don't know, Michael." A hesitant Eric Shrove

offered. "Justin was a friend of mine and although I agree with your ideas on brooding and life going on, I just don't feel up to it at the moment." Eric stood suddenly. "If you'll excuse me I'd like to go back to my room and lie down." Eric edged around the table. "I think too, I'll stay here tonight, Melody. Thank you all the same."

Ignoring Conran's entreaties, Eric hurried from the room.

"Curious man, that Mr. Shrove," said Conran watching the door slowly close.

"I was just discussing my room with Miss Pinklingill, Mr. Conran, and it reminded me . . ."

"Is everything okay?"

"Everything's fine." Winston ignored Sister Mary's pinched titter. "I was curious as to why Smelton built all those small rooms."

"For the Norse Society. The members stayed there the two weeks a year that they met. When we bought the castle the rooms were filled with straw and horsehair mattresses. The gentlemen involved obviously took it all very seriously."

"I see."

"And Winston, please call me Michael. No last names allowed here at the monastery."

"Mr. Wyc." Miss Pinkingill spoke in a low voice. "I wish to hear more about this historical preservation idea. What's involved . . . that sort of thing."

"Well, it's quite complex and the . . . eh . . . standards difficult to meet. The application process begins with filling out a survey form which is then mailed to the State Office of Parks, Recreation and Historic Preservation. This form includes physical and historical information about the site and why you believe it to be of significance."

"Are we significant, Michael?"

"Well . . ."

"It doesn't really matter what we think," said Winston quickly. "The county will send out a review committee to determine whether or not the castle warrants consideration. If they think it does, then they notify the State Review Board who sends down a professional review team. From here the application is forwarded to the Keeper of the National Register in Washington for yet *another* staff review. The Secretary of the Interior then signs the castle onto the list. This all takes a lot of time."

"My goodness," sighed Conran. Miss Pinkingill stared off at the peepholes.

"Do you have any Indian burial mounds on the property?" asked Winston.

Conran shook his head.

"Woolly mammoth bones?"

Another negative shake.

"If it means anything, the land cannot be sold or developed while the review process is in operation."

"Well, that's something, I guess."

Conran's cheerful countenance was fading. Winston wondered why, with Justin Barefoot gone, the process was still necessary. Somebody had removed the major critic. Or was there more involved?

"I think your best bet is to go with the local government."

"The town of Buddingville?" asked Miss Pinklingill.

"Sure. The town board along with the local historic society can designate protection for sites within the town's jurisdiction. This can offer as much protection as anything the feds can do unless of course the Army Corps of Engineers decides to build a dam here or widen the river."

"The town," said Conran rather wistfully.

"I would think the town would like to see this land stay the way it is. Keep the rural flavor. Does the monastery get along with the town fathers?"

"Sort of," said Conran.

"We ignore each other," said Miss Pinkingill. "I think it best we do the same with this whole idea, Michael. At least until the unfortunate events of the day have settled a little. Perhaps I could look into the local possibility. I do live here."

"I think that's a good idea," said Winston hoping that the process was over and he could forget about the Oblates of Tranquil Deliverance.

"Maybe," said a quiet Conran.

Miss Pinkingill made a show of taking her watch off the table, snapping it shut, and placing it back in her pocket.

"Heavens, where does the time go? Mr. Wyc, we shall expect you around nine-thirty. Our house is usually abed by the stroke of ten. We could probably all use a good night's rest. Don't you think?"

Winston caught the eye of a sullen Michael Conran.

"Miss Pinklingill thinks I would be more comfortable."

Conran glanced at Miss Pinklingill.

"I . . . I think it's probably a good idea." Conran didn't appear convinced.

"I bid you a good night then, Michael. Mr. Wyc, nine-thirty."

Winston could only nod, his head bobbing up and down like some lawn ornament in the wind. Sister Mary lost little time in getting Miss Pinklingill from the table to the door. The click-clack of her heels had just faded from the hall when the kitchen door flew open and Chef Carol burst upon Winston and Conran with a wheeled cart piled high with covered dishes. The surprised woman stopped halfway across the room, her head turning this way and that in search of extra mouths to feed.

"Oh damn," said Conran staring about the table, a man caught in battle with his gun empty. Winston wasn't sure but he thought he heard a laugh somewhere off in the hollows of the castle.

Chapter 11

Winston stood on the porch looking out over the lawn, his stomach so full that his breath came in fast, short gasps. And now his head had begun to hurt. Never had he eaten so much, so quickly, and under such duress. Chef Carol had been rather adamant in her food presentation. The two bowls of oatmeal soup had been fairly harmless and if left in the mouth for a short period, the bulgur grain balls broke down into a consistency almost malleable enough to swallow. But halfway through his second helping of Tempeh Royale, Winston had thrown all caution to the winds, saying offhandedly to Conran that he couldn't possibly eat any more "moldy tofu," calling it Distempeh Royale. The remark had its desired effect and Winston was forced to leave the table before the cook could find something large enough to hurt him. For all he knew, poor Conran was still back in the dining room finishing off the remaining dishes and apologizing profusely.

A walk was needed and Winston ambled out onto the lawn. Stopping a hundred yards from the porch, he turned to look back at Smelton Castle. In the fading light and from this angle the edifice looked more the stately home than the walled castle, the portico lending a definite calming effect on the structure as a fortification. The lancet windows of the other sides were replaced with oriel windows at the ground level and full, mullioned casements at the other floors. The only noticeable light was in the windows of the room over the library. Standing there, watching shadows move behind the curtains, Winston thought back on his earlier visit to that room. Someone had been there just before him, someone other than Sister Mary the Engine. It could have been staff possibly, but where had they gone? And all those nuns' habits. Winston had meant to ask about the nuns. If there were nuns about, then where might they be and what function did they fulfill at the retreat? And *who* was the funny man he'd met in the belvedere? These were all questions that at any other time Winston would probably not have bothered himself with, but since there had been a murder that day the usual became suspect and all shadows concealed the unspeakable. Speaking of the unusual, Eric Shrove seemed to be rather spooked himself. What could he have wanted to discuss so privately?

Very briefly Winston considered searching for Eric but ruled out that ambition when he realized he didn't have the heart or, for that matter, the stomach for such an adventure. Besides, with the coming night the darkened castle was beginning to look far too large and inhospitable for any casual exploration. Even the lengthening shadows that crept across the lawn had an eerie and malicious temper. Nothing like standing by oneself out among the dimming topiary, beneath the silhouette of a quieting, ill lit castle, to bring out the Gothic imagination. As Winston hurried toward the portico, slavering wolves watched from the trees, bats circled above his head.

In the few minutes it took Winston to race to the portico steps, the night was upon him. If it had not been for the dim lights of the entrance hall, he would have stood in complete darkness. Standing their calming his beating heart, Winston suddenly remembered his sleeping arrangements for the night: a comfortable evening spent with the Pinklingills. What could possibly have come over him to accept such an invitation? Checking his watch, he saw he had only forty minutes to cancel out. An image came to him of Miss Pinklingill and the Engine sitting up by the door and waiting for Mr. Wyc far into the night. They didn't look happy. Perhaps he'd better call.

As Winston went to enter, the dining room door swung open and a very unhappy Michael Conran lumbered into the hall. Winston stepped back into the shadows. A few trailing tethers and the man would have looked like a Macy's Thanksgiving Day parade float gone mean. Best to avoid Conran at the moment and let him sleep off his indigestion and bad humor. As Conran disappeared through the archway into the conservatory, Winston detected movement of still another figure; this time a nun coming down the stone staircase. Without knowing quite why, Winston was sure that this was the same person he'd spied watching him from the balcony at his arrival. As the nun approached the bottom of the steps Winston entered the hall.

"My goodness." The nun put a hand to her mouth. "You startled me, coming out of the dark like that."

"I'm sorry. I've been out watching the sunset."

"Are you a guest?"

"In a way, yes. I was here today delivering a sermon

on historic preservation and I've been asked to stick around. My name is Winston Wyc.''

"I'm Sister Kerry."

"I think I saw you earlier. Out at the front?"

Sister Kerry bowed her head. "That's possible."

The Sister seemed so genuinely embarrassed that Winston decided to let the matter drop.

"Look . . . I, eh . . . need to make a phone call. Do you think the office is still open?"

"Oh yes, of course. I'm heading there now to relieve Sister Catherine. Would you like to come with me?"

I sure would, thought Winston. Suddenly the castle was *full* of nuns. The wolves fell back into the night. Winston fell in behind.

"The office always has someone to personally answer the phone. Our clients can call anytime and be assured that someone will be here to talk to them. It helps."

"A voice in the night," said Winston.

"Exactly."

The conservatory was lit by small night lights hidden among the plants. Indirect lighting in the reception area gave that room the muted, anticipatory feeling that hospital lobbies have after regular hours. Sister Catherine looked like Sister Kerry's clone with her slight build and perfectly bland, pink face. The two nuns spoke softly to one another as Winston waited out by the refectory table. Sister Catherine hurried by, her head on her chin, her hands folded before her.

"You may use the phone now, Mr. Wyc."

"Thanks."

Chapter 12

Mary Bartlett did a perfunctory tidying up of the cottage, bending to swat at some dust, checking to see if sheets were clean, all the while trying not to spill her Jack Daniel's. She had just poured that drink and was readying herself for a long, hot bath when Winston Wyc called. At first she had considered saying no to his coming over, it had been a long day, but under the man's casual good humor she could detect a strong plea for rescue and she gave in. Besides, she reminded herself, he was the main witness to the year's hottest news story. *And* he was tall and cute and crumply looking. Just the way she liked them.

Standing on her small deck, Mary shut her eyes and let the sounds of the Hudson River with its cooling breeze relax and rejuvenate her tired body. Sighing loudly, she settled into a large Adirondack chair and waited for Winston Wyc to show. This was her favorite time of the day. Head back, drink in hand, daylight gone, listening to the strong quiet of the river as it flowed steady and unseen just beyond the railing. Only tonight, Mary's peace was disturbed by the memory of Justin Barefoot, murdered just a quarter of a mile down the river from where she now sat. What would Uncle Dutch say? Not to worry, he'd say, his leathery, old face getting all pensive and tight. He would remember what *his* father had told him, that the shame and outrage of the man's spirit was flowing away from her, working its way downstream. That its hate and need for revenge would not poison the waters around her cottage. Dutch's father would not have fished below that point where Barefoot was found, not wanting to catch or eat fish that had swum through the killing waters. Mary chuckled to herself. It was just the kind of thing the Dace family would still believe. Sipping at her drink, Mary let its woodsy-smell mingle with the odor of the river. Dutch said they were lucky to live this close to the Hudson for it allowed them to keep their drinks neat, the strong presence of water being enough to fill your glass without diluting the whiskey.

Hearing a car approach, Mary forced her mind back to the business at hand. Watching Winston Wyc climb her steps, she wondered if she should question him a little more closely on the murder or should she let it go and enjoy the evening? She decided to let him make the choice. If her reporting instincts were correct, and they usually were, he'd be the one who'd want to talk. She'd just listen.

Chapter 13

Winston felt at ease on Mary Bartlett's small deck. The closeness of the river and the cottage were a comfort as was the woman's good humor, her easy laugh skipping out over the water like a tightly tossed fishing line. Winston had brought a small pizza and a large bottle of wine and a desperate need to get clear of the Oblates of Tranquil Deliverance. Saying he was staying at friends, Miss Pinklingill had actually sounded relieved that he wasn't coming. As long as he was comfortable, she was happy. Winston would have been comfortable sleeping in his rented car, anything to avoid his castle cell and the numbing quiet of the eighteen inch thick walls.

"So you think it was one of the board members?" asked Winston. He'd promised himself he wouldn't discuss the murder, but the need for catharsis was great and he couldn't help coming back to it. At first he'd thought she was manipulating him, playing the reporter, but she had only sat there, neither encouraging or discouraging, only listening. By the last slice of pizza and the third glass of red wine, they were well into solving the mystery.

"It had to be. Who else would want to stop the sale of the land?"

"Sister Kerry? Some other nun? I don't know. Who else works there that might be upset if the monastery went co-op?"

Mary laughed. "Could have been a believer. Any guests staying there?"

"You mean deliverees? I didn't see any."

"That's right—deliverees. I'd forgotten that's what they're called."

"Wait a minute. I ran into a strange little guy up in one of the belvederes. Really odd looking. Especially the eyes. I haven't seen eyes like that since the days of hallucinogens."

Mary sat up. "Did he say who he was?"

"No. Why? Do you know who he is?"

Slowly shaking her head, Mary placed her drink carefully on the arm of her chair.

"What did he look like?"

"Bozo the Clown on drugs. Come on, you have some idea. I can see it in everything you're not saying."

"No, no . . . I'm . . . eh, just running back over the guests I've met up there. Bozo I'd remember."

Winston didn't believe her but he'd let it go for now. Tomorrow, back at the castle, he'd ask Conran about the man.

"By the size of the dining room, I'd say they had lots of deliverees showing up on the weekends."

"Lots. And all of them loaded. Not that they come up all the time, but when they need a little punishment that bastard Conran and his girls are ready."

"You mean the nuns?"

"The nuns." Mary smirked. "I've always wondered about that. I mean, who are these nuns and why in the hell would they have an order at the retreat? I can't believe any real church would associate itself in any way with that castle."

"I wondered that myself. Captain Sweetman didn't think the monastery had any religious tax deferment. Maybe they're Rent-a-Nuns."

"Yeah and maybe it's their time in hell."

"How many are there?"

"Not many. Five or six. You could ask Dutch."

"What about that Dace fellow? Could he be a suspect?"

"Dutch? Forget it. Dutch couldn't kill *anything*. Besides, if the retreat folded he could care less. There are people up and down the river who would hire Dutch at the drop of a sinker. He's the best fisherman from here to there. The best period."

"You like that guy a lot, don't you?"

"He's a good man and I respect him and what he believes in. He's been around a long time, lived his life the way he wanted and never been sorry. Not all of us can say that."

Winston wasn't sure. Dutch seemed to have a dark spot about him, something Winston couldn't put his finger on but that was definitely there. The face was a little too tight for the easy smile, the nonchalance too studied, the eyes a tad too quick. The man knew something and if he was as good as Mary believed then he probably didn't like what he knew. That could work against him if he wasn't careful.

"He said a funny thing when I knocked on his door the first time, the time I found Barefoot. I said something to the effect that I'd found this body in the water and Dutch said 'already?' Just like that. He was caught off guard I think, but when I said it was Barefoot he was genuinely surprised and I think he was upset."

"Oh yeah? What are you saying?"

"I'm saying I'm not so sure he didn't think someone else had popped up. Someone he *did* know about."

Mary was quiet. She had closed her eyes, her wine glass resting against her chin.

"I'm probably full of shit, right?" This was not the time to attack Mary's favorite old man.

"Could be." One eye pulled open. "You're right. Dutch may know something and if he doesn't want to talk about it then he has his reasons. But he didn't kill anyone."

Rising from her chair, Mary stepped into the living room. A moment later blues music floated back out to the deck, soft and plaintive and perfect. Mary reappeared with a bottle of Jack Daniel's and two towels.

"Hope you like Alberta Hunter. She's from down your way."

"Sounds nice."

Mary sat on the railing.

"Look . . . how about we drink a lot of this dark liquid, talk about something fun and go for a swim and . . . and who knows. Get to like each other," Mary suggested.

"Sounds good to me."

"What got you into this historian thing? You don't strike me as the bookish type."

Handing Winston a water glass of whiskey, Mary moved her chair next to his.

"My interest in architecture happened early." Winston took a sip. "My mother was a cleaning woman. She didn't really have to do it. I mean not many Irish women were still cleaning other people's homes by the time I was five years old, but she'd done it all her life and loved to be in wealthy houses, see the furniture, the big paintings, the rooms themselves. This was the only way she could do it and she used to take me along. If no one was there, she'd take me around the house, pointing out the different styles and periods of furniture, the heirlooms, how much everything was worth. She knew all this and wanted me to know too. I think she felt that if I was introduced to it early then I'd aspire to having the same myself someday."

Winston smiled to himself remembering the many opulent brownstones and apartments he'd visited as the cleaning lady's kid. Sitting in the kitchens, thumbing through magazines, being bored while his mother hummed in another room . . . and the cooks. Some were better than others but they all talked to him nonstop, not caring if he answered or listened, just happy to have someone to talk *at*, to be around, sneaking him cookies and saying how great his mother was at cleaning. These women were almost always black and Winston felt they were always a little surprised to see the white cleaning lady arrive.

"You aspire to grand things?"

"I'm afraid I'm a big disappointment to her on that score but I think she's happy I graduated and work with my head and not my hands. That was a big thing to her. How about you? You make Mom and Dad happy?"

"My father died in a fishing accident when I was twelve and Mom was never really around after that . . . I mean she was there, but she had to work two jobs to make ends meet. I look back on it though and it all seems okay somehow. I don't remember being abnormally unhappy."

"Your father fished the Hudson?"

"Sort of. His family had always been fishermen but by the time he could fish most of the Hudson was so polluted the feds wouldn't let you sell anything taken from the river except the shad, and that was seasonal. Soon as the water reached about fifty degrees the shad would show up to spawn. I could always tell because the shadbush would bloom with its tiny white flowers. I loved that time of year . . ." Mary took a long drink. ". . . it was the time of year my father would be around. He always came back to fish the shad with his family. March fifteenth to the end of May. They'd smoke shad fillets and sell them out of the back of the garage. People came from all over to buy those fillets." Mary took another long drink. "Other times my father worked the fishing boats off the coast of Long Island. Be out for a couple of months, come home for a few weeks, be gone again. . . . One day he never came back."

Winston and Mary sat listening to the river.

"Sorry," said Mary. "Didn't mean to be boring."

"Hardly. Nice to know the star reporter isn't tough all the way through."

Mary pointed at her head. "Feel this id, buddy. Like beef jerky."

Winston reached over and touched the side of Mary's head. The scalp felt oddly vulnerable under the soft, short hair. Winston stood to look out toward the river.

"You know, I've never been fishing. Commercial fishing makes sense to me but I've never understood the attraction of standing knee deep in cold water matching wits with something that has no brain. When I was a kid I used to think fish were headless. No kidding. The ones mom brought back from the market always had the head missing and I'd see them and wonder how they ate or talked to each other. I didn't want to eat them."

Laughing, Mary rose suddenly.

"You are full of shit, pal. How about a swim?"

Mary descended the steps to the water's edge. Pulling her shirt over her head, she looked back at him.

"This is no peep show, buddy. It's show and tell all around."

"I forgot my Jantzen's."

"Give me a break."

Winston sat on the bottom step removing his shoes. He couldn't remember the last time he'd gone skinny-dipping. In fact, he'd never been skinny-dipping. He wondered if the water was cold, if the fish would bite his thing. From behind, Mary looked like a tall boy, the thin, athletic body and short hair giving a lie to the very mature woman that turned to face him.

"Follow me. There's a float about fifty feet out and we can catch our breath and some moon rays. And stop looking so silly. Haven't you ever seen a naked woman before?"

"Not any as beautiful as the fisherman's daughter."

Mary smiled and shook her head. Turning, she took four steps and dove, the water parting gently to accept her. Winston waited for her head to reappear before leaping feet first into the dark.

"I've never made love on a float."

It was the first words spoken since Winston had jumped into the water. He now lay on his stomach staring into the water, his body and mind still warm and tingling. Mary, balanced on top of him, tried to keep her body off the splintery wood of the raft.

"Me neither," she whispered.

"What was that fancy arrangement with the ladder then?"

"Improvisation . . . I didn't want to get any splinters. You complaining?"

"Not this sailor."

"Good."

On reaching the float, Winston had found Mary waiting for him on the ladder, her legs pressed under her, her arms hugging her knees. At first she had placed her foot on his shoulder and wouldn't let him climb out of the water. Firmly removing her foot from his shoulder, he had brushed the instep with his lips and then tracing her leg with his mouth, he had risen from the water. There had been no hurry and no hunger. Their lovemaking had been as soft and as rhythmic as the river lapping gently against the wooden raft.

"I don't know if I have the energy to swim back," said Winston.

"Then I'll stay out here with you. I'll be your blanket from the cold."

"I wouldn't think of it." Winston was beginning to feel chilly. "You didn't by any chance bring that Jack Daniel's?"

"That's nice. Man prefers his whiskey to his woman. Did I hear you say your mother was Irish?"

Mary rose and without another word dove into the water. Winston watched until she disappeared in the dark before he followed.

Chapter 14

Still groggy from sleep, Winston only half-listened to Mary talking in the other room. He couldn't remember if he'd actually heard the phone or not, but Mary's sudden absence had aroused him.

"I gotta go, babe. There's another body."

Racing into the bedroom, a toothbrush stuck in her mouth, Mary began dressing hurriedly.

"What?" Winston was awake.

"Some environmentalists were dredging the river up under the New Holland Bridge looking for God knows what when they brought up this guy wrapped around an anchor."

"Another body? What time is it?"

"Guy hadn't been there too long. Couple of weeks maybe. Ehh . . . eight thirty. Should be able to ID the poor bastard."

"I was hoping you'd never put clothes on again."

"And what? Walk around crime scenes bare ass?"

"Why not?"

Bending down to kiss Winston on the forehead, Mary sat on the bed to put on her Reeboks.

"Look, I've got to get my buns on the road. I

noticed we left a slice of pizza out on the deck. Should be just right for breakfast. Bon appetite." Mary was out the door.

"Hey, wait a minute."

Tearing through the living room and leaping down the front steps of the cottage, Winston caught up with Mary's Pacermobile as she started up the drive.

"Not so fast. I have to go back to the City this afternoon and . . ."

"You ought to put some clothes on, Tarzan. Why is it that naked guys never look that great in the morning?"

Winston gave his birthday suit the once over.

"It's the knees."

"Why are you going back to New York?"

"I'm on vacation."

"Vacation. Where're you heading?"

"Well . . . actually, I don't ever leave the City. I take a room at the Sherry-Netherland."

"What kind of vacation is that? I thought you lived in New York."

"I do. I never leave the City to relax. Hotels are great. Your food is delivered to your door, there's a pool, although you have to wear a suit, and someone comes in every day and makes your bed. Plus you don't waste your time traveling. You should join me."

Mary laughed and shook her head.

"You're a piece of work, pal. Don't forget to vacuum before you leave."

Winston smiled at her retreating laughter. Back out on the deck, Winston considered the pizza and then a swim but abandoned both ideas for a hot shower and a stop at the local coffee shop before reentering the world of historical preservation. This morning his own preservation would take priority.

In the morning light the castle looked harmless, almost banal. Just a pile of crenelated stones that housed a handful of eccentrics and a homicidal maniac. Hopefully he would be putting it all behind him this afternoon. The Oblates of Tranquil Deliverance would have to go on without him. Conran stood in the reception area talking to Dutch Dace.

"Well, Winston I hope we enjoyed our night out."

Conran seemed friendly enough, his face back into its welcome mask.

"Old friends."

"I understood that to be the case. Had breakfast?"

Winston searched Conran's expression for any sign of irony but found none.

"Yes I have, thank you. Hi Dutch."

Dace only nodded.

"Seen the morning paper, Winston?"

"No."

"'Friends' have certainly grabbed the front page with our little problem."

Conran handed Winston the front section of the *New Holland Observer*. "Murder at Local Retreat" seemed to dominate the page. Winston would read it later when he felt stronger.

"*That* should be great for business," Conran snorted.

Or help it, thought Winston. Now the monastery could offer something for *all* the loonies.

"And you've certainly become popular, Winston. The phone is ringing off the hook. Claire has all the messages. We need to talk but I have a castle to run at the moment. Lunch?"

"Sure."

Conran heaved his weight from the reception room in the direction of the conservatory.

"How'd you like to take a ride on the boat?" Dace lit up a Camel.

"I'd love to. What time?"

"How about ten thirty. That's forty minutes. I have to give it a test run."

"I'll be there. Ohh, Dutch they found another body in the Hudson this morning."

Winston was impressed. Dace's eyes went dark for only a split second.

"River's been busy lately." Dace smiled.

"And Conran had assured me the Hudson was clean up this far."

"Yeah . . . well . . . ten thirty." Dace hesitated before turning to go. Winston was sure the man wanted to say something but then decided against it. The lanky frame stooped in the doorway for a moment before continuing.

"I hear you've got some calls for me." Winston wondered what time Claire came to work. Maybe the nuns had to be back in their cells before the sun rose.

"Three."

Claire handed Winston three pink memo sheets garnished with yellow smudges of egg salad. Sweetman had called wanting Winston to come to police headquarters at two that afternoon. Mary had called to say that the Sherry-Netherland sounded great. Would he want to wait a few days? He chuckled. Already he missed her. And the third was from someone he hadn't thought of in a long while: Dr. Janice Wetmore. The good doctor had been his pal and confidante through a pretty difficult period of his life—the dissolution of his romance with the lady from across the river. Janice considered herself something of an amateur sleuth and Winston decided to put that phone call on hold or she'd be over this side of the river making Captain Sweetman's life a misery. There was a possibility she'd show anyway. Janice and Melody would be a good pairing. Eric Shrove poked his head into the office.

"Oh Winston. I've been looking for you."

"Hi Eric. Have a good night."

"I took a pill the doctor gave me. How was dinner?"

Winston glanced at Claire. "I'll tell you about it later. What do you need?"

"Maybe we could go for a walk."

The two men exchanged pleasantries until they reached the end of the lawn where it dropped off to the river. It was the same spot where Winston had seen Barefoot plunge out of sight. Winston looked up the river to see if Mary's cottage was visible. A blip in the water might have been the float.

"Mr. Wyc, there's a few things going on here that I think you should know about because I feel they could have a direct bearing on this preservation issue."

Winston wasn't entirely sure he wanted to know. Eric's pudgy face had shrunken over night, the muscles around the mouth tight, his expression peevish. He looked like a spiteful little schoolboy about to turn in the whole class for calling him names.

"You can believe me, Winston, when I say I'm not a brave man and I'm probably putting myself in peril, but I feel I owe it to Justin."

Contorting his face into a pained expression, Eric took a deep breath and prepared his being for the no return journey into danger.

"I'm only an accountant and I've spent my life pretty much indoors . . ." Thinking back over his sedentary ways, Eric shook his head. ". . . and how I ever let myself get mixed-up in this mess I'll never know. Justin convinced me, I guess."

Winston checked his watch. Twenty-five minutes to the boat ride.

"If you'll bear with me a moment, I'd like to present first a little history. I was Justin's accountant for nearly fifteen years. Ten years ago he came to me to say that he was investing some monies in a castle in New York State. I was horrified of course, but once he explained his reasoning I had to agree."

"What was his reason?"

"The art work. You see Justin had just begun collecting Hudson River School painters at that time and Smelton Castle was full of paintings. That particular art colony was not so popular at the time and Justin saw a chance to pick up some great values for . . . really nothing. Gifford, Hetzel, Inness and even a few Churches, I believe. The people who approached Justin said that if he invested a certain amount, which was a large part of the cost, he could have all the paintings."

"How much did he invest?"

"A million and a half dollars. It was almost two-thirds of the selling price."

"Who approached him?"

"Michael and Cynthia."

"Cynthia?"

"Yes. The two knew somehow that Justin was looking for these particular painters. I guess it's a

133

small art world, and convinced him to come in on the deal." Eric grinned a wicked little grin. "Justin was no fool, though."

"What do you mean?"

"Justin didn't use *his* money." Eric gave Winston a triumphant little smile.

"Whose money did he use?"

"Justin got in touch with some people he knew in Washington that were looking for a good investment and convinced them to buy Smelton Castle and its property. A million and a half for one thousand acres along the Hudson was a good deal even then."

"Wait a minute. You're saying that Justin was fronting for these people?"

"That's right."

"And no one here knew that?"

Eric shook his head no.

"So he was killed for no reason. I mean . . . can't these people just send someone else to represent them?"

"It's possible, yes."

Staring out over the river, Winston tried fitting all this new information into a sensible paragraph. It was possible that the retreat people knew nothing about Justin's other investors. All the buyers aren't needed on any selling or deed transactions as long as Justin had a paper stating his authority to sign. If the money had been funneled through his own organization, then the deal would have remained secret. As long as the money is there, what does the seller care? And the title company is really working for the buyer . . . so there was a good chance the investors stayed out of the picture.

"I take it the investors knew nothing of the paintings." Eric nodded that they didn't. "Pretty smart.

134

Justin uses someone else's money to buy all these works of art."

"The investors came away with a good deal in the property."

"But it was an investment, right? At some point the group was going to want to sell the property. I take it that time had come."

"It would seem so." Eric gave a shrug.

"A company was mentioned in the library yesterday."

"Shumway and Associates. They're a big development group from Baltimore. They've offered over ten million for the property."

"Whoa, doctor. Why doesn't the retreat take the deal? Seems with that kind of money they could relocate pretty easily."

"Because they don't have that large an investment. Justin's group had put up most of the money, remember?"

It still didn't make sense. Killing Barefoot wouldn't necessarily mean stopping a sale. What if the man was in extreme debt? Or had greedy relatives?

"Do you know who killed Mr. Barefoot?" Winston confronted Eric.

Eric took in another big breath but it only seemed to make his face tighter.

"No I don't."

"Could you make an educated guess?"

Eric adamantly shook his head no. If the man knew, he wasn't about to put his head on the block. Suddenly Eric grabbed Winston's arm for support, his eyes fixed on a spot down the hill.

"What's the matter?" Winston searched the bushes but saw nothing.

"Oh gosh."

Turning, Eric spied Conran coming toward them behind the wheel of a golf cart. He began to talk quickly.

"Listen, Winston . . . you have to find Thomas Smelton."

"The former owner of the castle? What do you mean find him? How do I do that?"

"He's here. Living in the castle."

"He is?"

"Yes. There's another castle sort of tucked into the one we see. Smelton lives there."

Winston realized his mouth was hanging open and closed it.

"Why don't *you* find him?"

"I've . . . I've tried. Look, you're the architectural historian, you know about such things. You find Thomas and I guarantee we can save this property from development."

"Shouldn't I just tell the police?"

Eric looked genuinely hurt. "Winston, I thought you'd be more fun than that."

"Fun? There's people being killed, Eric."

"Listen . . . don't mention this conversation to anyone until we talk again. This place is full of crazies and unless we find Thomas he's going to wind up dead too." Eric wrangled his face into a shield of desperation. *"Pleeeease."*

Winston didn't know what to say. There was much too much going on, too much information coming his way, and now the surfacing of one Thomas Smelton.

"I don't know *what* to say."

Covering the lawn quickly, Conran pulled up beside them.

"Hello, hello. I've been looking for you, Eric. You have a phone call."

"I do?"

"No other Eric Shrove's here I believe. They said it was urgent. Here's the number."

Eric studied the pink memo slip.

"It's a Washington exchange but I don't recognize the number."

"Come along. I'll give you a ride."

Eric looked at Winston.

"You want me to come with you?"

Yet another deep breath from Eric.

"No, no. You'll be late for your appointment. Maybe we can get together for lunch."

"He's having lunch with me." Conran gunned the cart's engine.

"Oh. Well, maybe after lunch?"

"I'm afraid I'm to meet with Captain Sweetman. Actually I may not be here for lunch either." Winston shrugged at Conran.

"Then for tea. We can all meet for tea and talk about the inner child. Do you believe children are innately good, Winston?"

Winston could only shake his head up and down.

"That evil is sickness, not sin?"

"I'll . . . eh, give it some thought."

"Good. Come Mr. Shrove."

Winston watched as the cart began a wide circle and headed back toward the portico, Conran waving his arm in the air in a grand parting gesture.

Chapter 15

The area below the New Holland Bridge had once been a home for transients. The railroad station lay in the shadow of the bridge, providing a sheltered and convenient spot for rest overs. Mary could remember being out on the water at night as a young girl and seeing their campfires, the glow throwing eerie shadows on the cement bridge supports. Since then the city fathers, in an attempt to attract business to New Holland, had had the area cleaned up and turned into a park. That is, they crisscrossed the site with sidewalks, planted some dead trees, and scattered about metal benches that were unbelievably uncomfortable. Now it was an *attractive* place for transients to rest over. No one else ever used the park except young boys who fished from the stone promenade and, at night, lovers with no home of their own.

Leaning against an iron railing, Mary watched the bag boys zip up their bundle of death. A rope and anchor, which had accompanied the dead man to the bottom, sat near him in a pool of water. Captain Sweetman hadn't appeared but just about every other cop was present, running this way and that, looking for the tenth time into the river, viewing the body, talking to the environmentalists. Mary's fellow media bums hurried after the cops. She wandered over to inspect the anchor.

"Well, well if it ain't Mr. Bartlett."

Sergeant Jones stood with two other policemen guarding the anchor.

"When are we going to stop the bullshit, Jonesy. It's old."

"I know it gets to you, that's all. Nothing personal, Mary dear."

"Yeah, well maybe I'll write an article on cops and sexual harassment. Nothing personal, Jonesy dear."

"What sex? Give me a break."

Jones huffed away in disgust.

"Hi Freddy." Mary addressed the younger of the two officers.

"Hi Mary. Don't be upset with Sarge. He don't mean nothing."

"Don't count on it. This the weight?"

"Yeah. It had been strapped across the back with the rope there. Left some nice dents in the guy. He probably would have never come up except the State guys there ran into him taking bottom samples. Damn near broke their little dredger."

"Yeah, I talked to them for a minute. They seem pretty shook."

"It's not the kind of pollution they was looking for." The two men laughed.

"Anybody know who the pollution is?"

"He's not been in the water but a couple of days, maybe a week but it's hard to tell. He still ain't in all that great a shape."

"No wallet or anything?"

"Not that we found right off."

"Nice size anchor. Must have dropped him from the Queen Mary."

Mary leaned down to inspect the anchor closer.

"Don't touch it."

"I won't."

Looking for identification marks, Mary could find none. Sometimes the name of a boat was stamped into its anchor. This didn't seem to be the case here, although not being able to see the other side, it was difficult to know. It must have been a large boat, though. This particular anchor would have to be used for a forty footer or more, thirty-five to forty-five thousand pounds. There weren't that many boats that size in the neighborhood. Of course it could have come from anywhere up or down the river.

"Okay, guys. Let's load this baby up."

A police truck with a winch had pulled up alongside them and Sergeant Jones had climbed out to supervise the loading.

"Recognize the anchor, *Msss*. Bartlett?"

Mary had to grin. "Can't say I do, Sergeant Jones. You recognize that body?"

"Can't say I do, *Msss*. Bartlett. Sorry we can't stand around and make copy with you. We got a job to do."

"Always nice to see my tax dollars at work. Take care gentlemen."

Wandering back over to the railing, Mary gazed into the Hudson. Maybe Winston had been right. That anchor could certainly belong to the monastery's boat, it was big enough, and if what Winston had said concerning Dutch was true, then maybe this was the body. But what could Dutch be doing that involved dead people? In his younger days it might have been a possibility, but not now. The temper was gone and Mary knew that Dutch wanted to glide into

140

his older age with no worries and no obligations. How had he put it: a fishing line in the water with no bait and no hook. Besides, this anchor had never been used. It was new. Not a bit of paint missing, not a scratch, no chain burns.

Turning, Mary found she was the only one left except two boys who stood staring at the spot where the body had lain. Walking back to the Pacermobile, she scheduled her day. First she'd visit a few marine sales, then go back to the paper and write her story. Then she'd check in with Roberta. Roberta was a woman cop who liked to tell tales and she belonged to Mary's support group. Tonight there was a meeting and an advance phone call could garner plenty of info regarding this anchor and its pal. That should take her up to dinner and possibly some time with her new friend Winston Wyc. It would be a full day.

Chapter 16

Winston watched Dutch pilot the boat out into the middle of the river. The engines rumbled deep and powerfully under them, a volcano about to erupt. Dace had seemed reluctant to be friendly when Winston had arrived, as though he wanted to put a distance between them. Standing on the dock, Winston had wondered if Dace was being ordered to perform the role of caretaker or if he was feeling strange about the appearance of this new dead man. Either way, Winston had had second thoughts about being out on the water with a man who so obviously didn't like the idea. A string of surly monotones would get old quickly. Oddly enough, the minute they left the dock, Dace's attitude changed. Once out on the river the man had appeared relaxed, in control, his manner affable. Whatever the reasons for the remoteness, those concerns vanished once Dace felt the water under him.

Winston had never been in a boat this large and was amazed at the authority he felt riding in its pilot-house. The river seemed less broad, less intimidating, its currents and cold depths under control. Nothing could happen on a boat this size. One was safe.

"I'm going up river about a quarter of a mile . . ." Dace shouted back to Winston. ". . . and drop anchor."

Winston moved closer. "Why's that?"

"I've put the anchor on a new chain and I need to run it out and rewind it. You can help."

"Okay."

Settling into a cushioned seat, Winston let the warm wind blow his hair and watched the passing shoreline, the wind and watery distance giving him a comfortable feeling of detachment as if a tether had been cut. And not just a physical distance but an emotional and psychological detachment that, instead of threatening, brought him a sense of calm and relief. Maybe it was this same feeling that Dace enjoyed and that allowed him to relax. Winston had once been given a gift of one hour in a sensory deprivation tank and after surviving the first five minutes of panic, he had relaxed and enjoyed the experience. That same feeling of serenity now washed over him and, although his senses were being bombarded, he felt that same calm, that same peacefulness. Had he been standing on a mountain top, far removed from anything or anyone, the effect would not have been the same and he realized it was from being out on the river. It was what the two entirely different moments held in common: the water and its support, that feeling of being released from the earth, from the restraint of gravity. No wonder the stories and songs told of crossing water to get to Heaven. Of course, Barefoot might be of a different opinion. The engine noise suddenly quieted.

"This is a good spot. Deep and out of the way," said Dace.

The bubble of serenity burst. How was he to interpret Dace's curious grin? Gazing out at the

143

distant shore, Winston realized he was alone and vulnerable, that his good health and happiness were in the care of this man with the dark eyes and questionable purposes. That this same distance made him an easy target.

"I need for you to go down to the bow, undo the anchor, and drop it overboard."

Leaving the pilothouse, Winston edged along the deck to the bow. Dace nodded at him to continue out to the anchor. Winston looked into the swirling water and over to the shore and speculated on the success of swimming that span. The odds weren't good. Hearing a noise below him, Winston had a fleeting image of someone else lurking aboard the boat. Nothing like a recent murder to keep the paranoia fine-tuned.

The anchor was secured to the deck by a hasp which Winston released. With considerable effort he lowered the anchor over the side. A small engine whined beneath him as the anchor began a controlled fall into the water. Dace motioned for Winston to join him in the salon.

"Thanks."

"No problem."

Dace took some bags out of a small refrigerator.

"I packed some lunch. Hungry?"

"Lunch? Sure." Winston was surprised at Dace's thoughtfulness. Whatever was bothering him must not have anything to do with himself.

"Beer or whiskey?"

"Beer would be nice. Little early for me on the whiskey."

"That's the part about getting old I like. You survive this long, what the hell, enjoy your damn self. You know, I gave up smoking for twenty long years, some doctor said it would kill me. But on my

144

sixty-fifth birthday I lit up a Camel and I haven't quit since. So I lose a few months. I could go at any time now and not regret my passing."

Well I've still got a few months left, thought Winston. And a man who hits the whiskey in the middle of the day doesn't usually do so because he *can* but because something *bothers* him.

The two men settled into the cushioned benches that lined the rear deck of the boat. Setting the bottle of Jack Daniel's on the floor between his legs, Dace took a baguette, a tube of smoked sausage, and a block of cheese from the bags. They sat in silence as Dace sliced off pieces and arranged them on the flattened paper bags. Winston drank his beer and decided he could relax once again.

"New Holland here used to send boats out all over the world. Was big in the whaling trade at one time."

"Whaling? Seems a long way from the ocean."

"Not too far. This strip of river takes you straight there. Boats were safe up here from the English, and the local farm boys would hire on cheap, wanting to see the world. Many a farm was bought with money saved by boys who went to sea and came back men. Seen much of the world?" asked Dace.

"Not much. When you're brought up in New York you tend to think that *is* the world."

"I was in the Merchant Marines for twenty years. Was around the world a couple of times myself. It can change your outlook on things."

"How's that?"

"Different people, different cultures, different politics. Sometimes it works on the way you think. Changes you."

Listening to Dace, Winston wondered where the conversation was going. Did he want to change Winston's viewpoint or was he going to offer an explanation for recent events?

"See that bridge?" Dace poked a piece of sausage in the direction of the New Holland Bridge. "Wasn't there when I was a kid. Used to be you could see all the way from Danskammer Point to Crum Elbow without seeing nothing but Hudson River and its banks. People have forgotten." Dutch changed gears. "That's about twelve miles. The early river captains called it Long Reach. There's a term for a historian."

"A reach?"

"Some still use it. It's a stretch of water where you can see clearly from one spot to another. Man can go the entire stretch with one setting of his sail usually. Back when sail and steam was the power the river was divided into reaches."

"They're using ferry boats again down in Manhattan. Got one in the East River and one or two in the Hudson."

"At one time, everything had to cross the river by boat. We couldn't have been sitting where we are now fifty years ago. Too much river traffic. And ferries. Hell, we used to sit down here and watch the cars pile up to load on the *Brinckerhoff* on weekends. A hundred and fifty cars would line up for that damn ferry. They'd have to wait two hours." Dace smiled his wire smile. "The *Brinckerhoff.* Haven't thought of that one for a long time. One hundred and eleven feet. Stopped running in '41. What a beauty." Dace took a long pull on the whiskey. "And paddle steamers. A few survived up to my day. The best was the *Mary Powell,* long and white she was, with a bell that sounded like silver coins dropping into a crystal glass. That sound comes back to me sometimes." Dace broke from his reverie. "Know much about the Hudson?"

"Just the obvious. What a landlubber learns in history books."

Dace nodded and looked back over the river. Winston wanted Dutch to keep talking, to tell what he knew.

"I'm afraid my history doesn't venture much further than the tip of Manhattan. I know the Dutch opened up the Hudson with the beaver trade and the English looking for pitch for their warships," Winston contributed.

"That's a lot of it. Pine trees and beavers." Dace chuckled. "They sent the beaver pelts back to the old country to be made into hats and coats for the Russians. The Ruskies couldn't get enough beaver coats. They didn't have any water-slappers in that part of the world. But the big profits came in beaver cods."

"Beaver cods? Sounds like a hairy fish."

"Not far off. Cods was their word for balls. Beaver balls were supposed to cure everything. They'd put them in a pouch so you could smell them. Claimed to cure idiocy and lameness among other things. Many ships sailed from this region with their holds full of nothing but beaver balls."

"You're kidding."

"Some of the old timers say the beavers got wise at one point and used to castrate themselves with their teeth, leave the cods out for the hunters so they'd leave the rest of the animal alone."

Winston laughed. "How long since you got out of the Merchant Marines?"

"Retired about twelve years ago. Job's been going to the Asian boys and the Arabs for some time. U.S. stopped shipping really. Cost too much, I guess. Was hard to ship out unless you wanted to connect up

147

with one of the oil companies." Dace took his time lighting up a Camel. "Came back to the River."

The two men enjoyed the sun on their faces. "What a day," said Winston. "Where's the name *Hyorky* come from? Indian?"

Dutch shook his head. "Nope. No one remembers really. Comes from way back, maybe English, the seventeenth century. It's the place every sailor looks for, that island of milk and honey where the food drops from the trees and the women are all beautiful."

"I can imagine in seventeenth century England that would have been a real reason to go to sea."

"Any century, Cap."

Winston watched Dutch take another drink. "How's working for the monastery?"

"Has its moments." Dace rose. "Almost twelve-thirty. Let's see if this anchor wants to come back aboard."

"Thanks for lunch."

Dace grunted something and headed back up to the pilothouse. The friendly part of the trip was over. Winston went forward to catch the anchor.

The ride back to the boathouse was made in silence as if Dutch had talked himself out for the day. Winston didn't mind. Relaxing against the gunwale, he enjoyed the scenery, thought of beaver cods and Mary Bartlett. Maybe he wouldn't go back to the City right away. Moon rays and night swims had begun to sound better than room service and cable TV.

As the towers of Smelton Castle appeared above the trees, Winston moved down to the lower deck. Maybe he could take a secure line onto the dock. The foliage along the shore was dense but at one section it opened up and Winston could see a nun sitting on the bank smoking a cigarette. Having been raised a Catholic, Winston knew that some nuns smoked, but the image had always bothered him, as if the sanctified had been corrupted by the profane. Winston's father had a life of few pleasures but his Sunday afternoon cigar was so important that his mother had learned to say nothing and confined her tight-lipped rantings to the kitchen for the hour it took Mr. Wyc to finish defiling, not only the backyard, for the house was off-limits, but the entire ecological food chain. With his father's unabashed joy offset by his mother's mumbled entreaties for the Virgin's intervention, Winston grew up with understandably ambiguous feelings toward the subject. The occasional Sunday visit was now almost always strained by his father inviting him out back for an hour of smokey male bonding. Winston knew his mother would have to be watching from Heaven's gate before he could ever accept the proffered H. Upmann.

Glancing back to the pilothouse, Winston could see that Dace was staring at the nun and that the nun's presence upset him, his face having become grim and rigid. Quickly, Dace was past Winston and onto the dock where he secured the boat.

"Come with me."

Dace took Winston forcibly by the arm and led him away at a trot up the hill toward the castle. Once out of sight of the boathouse he stopped.

"Listen to what I have to say. Go back to New York and forget about this place."

"What's going on?"

Dace glanced back down the path before speaking low and directly into Winston's startled face.

"That world I mentioned earlier is full of things that no longer require any explanation. Go back to New York."

Dace motioned for Winston to get going and then he was gone; his long, leathery profile stopping for one more glance before he disappeared. Hurrying up the path to the castle, Winston hesitated at the edge of the lawn. Was there something he had failed to notice or was it the nun herself that had prompted the reaction from Dutch? Maybe Dutch had problems with smoking nuns himself. Winston doubted it, but Dutch's advice to skip town would not have to be repeated. The longer Winston stayed around the Oblates of Tranquil Deliverance, the less tranquil the damn place seemed. Health food, secretive nuns and murder were all too rich for Winston's blood and then there was Eric Shrove rambling on about the mysterious Thomas Smelton the Umpteenth. Winston came up short. Staring up at the castle roof, he realized that that must have been the old man he'd run into up in the belvedere, the one with the faraway eyes. If that *was* Tom Smelton, then what in the hell was he doing still at the castle and why did Eric need help in finding him? Sitting on the grass, Winston thought over his options. He was to meet with Captain Sweetman in forty minutes and after that he could flee. The Captain would certainly love to hear about all Winston had been through since their last conversation. Or he could keep his mouth shut, sign his original deposition, and *then* flee. Or he could help Eric find this Smelton fellow and try, by himself, to make sense out of it all . . . or he could forget everything and just hide out in Mary's cottage until she got tired of him. The last option did have its appeal, but this Smelton thing was beginning to bother him. Why was the man still here, living in the castle? It didn't make sense unless. . . .

Rising, Winston avoided the portico and walked around the castle to the main entrance. Neither

Conran nor Shrove were on his list at the moment for something to do. Hurrying through the main gate, Winston waved at Claire's hidden camera, crossed the cobblestones and jumped into his rented Cougar. He would make a decision as he rode into New Holland. Would he be smart and let the police find Mr. Smelton and probably the answers to this mystery or would he be bold and take a chance on becoming the Hudson River's next underwater ornament? Ahhh, life in the country. Never a moment's peace.

Chapter 17

Everett Whaley stood back from the engine he was working on and stared at Mary over his half-glasses. Taking a rag from his rear pocket, he took his time wiping his hands and thinking about Mary's question.

"Why don't you ask Dutch?"

"He wanted me to pick it up but I forgot. I thought if it was still here I'd give him a surprise."

Everett peered over Mary's shoulder at the Pacer-mobile and then back at the rag moving in his hands. "You'd planned on taking it away in that thing?"

"Well . . . no, I was going to borrow a truck. Is it here?"

"Dutch already come and got it. A month ago. You're a little late, Mary." Everett stuck the rag back into his pocket and headed slowly across the yard to his shop. Everett Whaley owned and operated the New Holland Marine Sales and Service located on the Hudson a short distance north of the city. He was third generation in the business and was known by all the local fishermen and boaters who'd been around that long themselves. Whaleys, as it was known, didn't advertise, and if you were new in the area you probably would never be able to find it. Everett liked it that way. Too damned much business as it was, he'd mutter to anyone willing to listen. Before you knew it he'd have to hire several new people and good ones didn't exist. If you were looking for a new deck chair for your boat or something that found fish electronically, then Everett's marine sales was not for you. He repaired boat engines and sold bait but if one of the old timers needed something, like an anchor, then he'd use his office to purchase that something and pass along the percentage cut. If Mary's family hadn't been coming in here for three generations themselves, Everett Whaley wouldn't have even looked up when she entered his boatyard.

"Here it is." Everett pulled a greasy sheet of paper from a stack on his counter. "Picked it up May fifteenth. Been here a while before that. Funny . . . he never mentioned you might be coming by."

"Dutch is getting old. He forgets things." Mary smiled.

"I'll let him know that, next time he comes by. Us old people like it when youngsters set us straight." Everett smiled back.

"Thanks Everett."

Entering her copy into the computer, Mary Bartlett watched the story begin its electronic journey to the newsroom and thought about what she had written. Around her, other reporters were doing the same, getting their articles into the big machine before deadline. If you discounted the clap-clap of the printers, it was the only time the room was ever quiet, everyone being so intent on ending their day.

The man found in the Hudson River was a

mystery, at least to the New Holland police. With no identification on his person, it was going to be difficult to ID the guy unless someone came forward looking for a missing person or somebody in the police organization recognized him. None of which had happened. Usually people missing were reported within a few days and this guy, according to the coroner, had been in the water for at least five to seven days, and still nobody had registered a complaint. There was a good chance he might have been brought to the river from a distance and dumped, although killers didn't often carry their victims very far from the scene of the murder. Another option was to take fingerprints, note identifying scars or tattoos, and send them out over the wire. Many a body had been ID'd in this way. Roberta would let her know if any information came back.

Roberta. What was Mary going to do about Roberta? They had met at a support group meeting and Mary, not being one to let an opportunity escape, had immediately begun exploiting Rob's hatred of her job and of police*men* to extract inside info. But now Rob had decided to come forward and raise a stink about male cops and their treatment of women. She wanted Mary to write an exposé for the *New Holland Observer*, to rake the bastards over the media coals. Mary wasn't quite sure about Rob's complaints which seemed to be more cathartic ravings then well observed misconduct. As near as she could make out these men in uniform were being what they were: *men*. Which certainly didn't excuse their conduct but, for Mary, explained a lot. Unless they became abusive, you accepted the fact and went on your way. For Mary to start writing headlines denouncing cops for being assholes would be the first step in ending her newspaper career in New Holland.

That is, if her boss, the all-American Matt Laird, would allow such an attack. Mary on the whole liked police officers. They had a rough job, and if it turned some of them into Attilla the Hun, most of the guys were all right and some of them actually gave a damn. But then she didn't work with them every day. Which raised the question as to why Rob continued to do so. All was grist for the support group. Mary wouldn't be there herself if she had all the answers.

Outside, the day was warm and friendly, the kind of afternoon where a park bench could be home for a few hours. Particularly if you had someone to share the bench. This Winston Wyc was going to be a problem. It had been some time since Mary's heart had softened toward a member of the opposite sex. She knew a good part of his attraction lay in the fact that he was a transient in her life, that they were connected in a sense to a horrific situation that underscored their relationship, made it seem more important than it might actually be. That all made sense. What didn't make sense was the fact that she liked him. She liked the fact that their whole affair so far seemed a complete surprise to him, that for each turn in their relationship he was genuinely startled. Not that he didn't care, he just wasn't expecting it. She found him ingenuous but not naive, spontaneous but not devious. Most men who wound up at her place spent the first half of the evening suggesting a midnight swim and the second half trying to dull her wits with alcohol. She hadn't found a man yet who could drink her under the table but they all had to give it a try. Winston was like Dutch in that respect. Alcohol was used to loosen the conversation, not the zipper. And maybe that was it, the fact that she didn't feel competitive or defensive in his presence. Whatever the reasons, the bottom line was she wanted to

155

see him again . . . and then again.

But right now she needed to see Dutch, or more exactly, his boat. If Mr. Dace had bought a new anchor she wanted to see it. Thinking back over the many years she'd known him, Mary couldn't recollect a time when she thought he might have lied to her. It wasn't a trait Dutch had in him. Evasive yes, dishonest no. Justin Barefoot being killed because he wanted to sell the retreat property was too simple. There had to be more to it for someone on the board to put themselves out on a limb like this. And if it wasn't somebody on the governing board, then it most definitely had to be someone connected intimately with the monastery and *known* by someone on the board. If what Winston had said was true, maybe Dutch was involved in something and maybe that something was the real reason Justin Barefoot wound up fish food.

On her way over to the retreat, Mary decided not to bother Rolly but to go directly to her place and take her outboard up to the boathouse. That way the chance of alerting someone to her presence was minimized and she could check for the anchor before arousing Dutch's suspicions. Mary couldn't get the Pacermobile to her cottage fast enough.

Chapter 18

Not until he had begun to read his deposition in Captain Sweetman's office did Winston know in which direction he was going to proceed: he would wait one more day before giving Thomas Smelton to the police. There would be another afternoon exploring Smelton Castle and another night with Mary, not that either acquaintance should end there. The mysterious Thomas Smelton had piqued his curiosity and Winston believed he knew how to find the man. If he could do that without causing a stir, the process should be safe. How dangerous could a few hours rambling around the castle be? Ask Justin Barefoot. Winston suppressed the thought.

"You might be interested to know that I followed through on some of your suggestions, Mr. Wyc."

Captain Sweetman sat unmoving at his desk watching and waiting. Today he was casually immobile in a white shirt with no tie, a pink alpaca sweater and dark, pleated slacks. To Winston, the Captain appeared to have that "afternoon of golf" look.

"My suggestions?"

"I had Bensen go over to the town clerk and look up the deed papers on the monastery sale. It was all pretty straightforward except for a covenant rider at the end."

"Yeah?"

"It would seem the property can't be sold or subdivided as long as the original owner is still alive."

"Tom Smelton."

"That's right."

"Hmmm."

"Barefoot must have known that, yet from what I understand, he was pushing to sell the property."

"I don't know . . ." said Winston. "Unless he thought he could get around the covenant. It *can* be done."

"Or maybe he thought Mr. Smelton had passed away."

Barefoot must have known that the man was alive because Eric Shrove knew. Winston sat silent.

"I thought for a moment that that might be the case," said Sweetman. ". . . but I got Mr. Smelton's lawyer's name off the deed and paid him a visit this morning. The man said that to the best of his knowledge his client was still alive. As to his whereabouts, he didn't know." Sweetman hesitated. "Or wasn't telling."

Glancing about, Winston offered a halfhearted shrug.

"Anyway, this lawyer said that, at least where the money was concerned, Barefoot, or rather Barefoot and Associates, seemed to be running the show. We're checking Washington now to find out who his associates are and whether or not they have any legal recourse with the death of Barefoot."

Winston tried to mirror the statue-like posture of the Captain but found he couldn't do it. Talking without gestures was impossible and when he thought he might begin to laugh, he abandoned the game altogether.

"Well, this deposition seems correct," said Winston.

"Good."

"Any other questions?"

The Captain took a moment to answer.

"No. You planning on heading back to the City?"

"Ummm . . . tomorrow. I'm not sure the retreat wants or needs my services any more, but I'd like to research the castle this afternoon and there's someone locally I want to see tonight."

"Be careful around the castle." The captain finally leaned forward. "Oh by the way, I received an interesting phone call this morning from a friend of yours."

"You did?"

"A colleague of mine over in Wistfield. Captain Andrews. Said he saw your name in the paper."

"What did he say?" Captain Andrews had once saved Winston's life. It had been only two years ago but it seemed like a hundred.

"Said you were innocently connected with some murders near Wistfield a few years back. Said you had a habit of keeping information to yourself. Is this true?"

"I . . . well . . . there had been a problem in Wistfield because someone had asked me not to reveal what I knew. It was stupid and almost got me killed."

"Uh huh."

The Captain waited. Winston realized his silly

grin was not enough.

"You've been there almost two days, Mr. Wyc, you must have heard something you could pass on. I seem to remember you wanted to be the detective."

"Well . . ." Winston quickly sifted through his information. "I might be repeating what you already know, but . . . Barefoot put up the money for the estate in return for the paintings that hung in the castle at the time. He was a collector. Conran and Cynthia Shea had approached him some years back with the proposition."

"Yes?"

"I know a company from Baltimore, Shumway and Associates, had made an offer of ten million dollars for the property . . ."

Holding up his hand for Winston to slow down, Sweetman began to take notes.

"I'm glad I asked." Sweetman's tone was colored with more than a little sarcasm. "Who told you this?"

"The board member, Eric Shrove. He's Barefoot's accountant from Washington and was placed on the board by Barefoot to keep an eye on the monastery's finances."

"What else did Mr. Shrove tell you?"

"Not much, other than that he admired Barefoot and was dumbfounded by his murder."

"Any of the other board menbers *not* admire Barefoot?"

"Enough to kill him? I don't know. I haven't really talked to the others."

The two men stared at each other.

"That's about it. Did you find the murder weapon?" asked Winston.

Sweetman took a moment to answer. "Yes, I think

we did. Lab is going over it now. Mr. Barefoot was struck by a club taken from the dining hall.''

"The dining hall?"

"Correct. And that's where we found it, hanging in its old spot. Fortunately, it hadn't dawned on the killer to clean it thoroughly."

"That sort of does away with the passing boat theory."

"I would say so." Sweetman rose and extended his hand. "Like I said, Mr. Wyc, be careful up at the castle this evening and a safe journey back to New York. Good luck. Hopefully you'll be hearing from us soon."

"I hope you get your man. I . . ."

"Yes?"

"Nothing."

Outside, Winston stood for five minutes on the police station steps chastising himself for being so dumb. What was it in his psychological makeup that made him want to pursue this Smelton character and possibly put his own life in danger? Any normal person would tell Captain Sweetman what he knew, get back in his rented car, and head home. But not Winston, who saw Smelton as a direct link to the past, a man who hid behind a screen of history, who could provide him with a tour of the castle about which Conran knew nothing. Winston wanted to see the old ledgers and guest books, to read letters and diaries, to study the minutiae that ran the castle in its heyday. Edifices were built of other than just wood and stone and Winston was sure that Thomas Smelton still kept all this at hand, hidden with him behind the sliding walls and peepholes. The man may have gambled his life away but the castle meant something to him and he had done what he had to do to keep it around him. It was a barrier against that world outside the shard-topped brick wall that defined his kingdom, a world he probably knew or cared nothing about. Winston wanted to spend some time in Smelton's world before it tumbled away.

Chapter 19

Having parked at a point along the retreat driveway, Winston walked the manicured lawn until he found a bench on which to sit and plan his late afternoon. Relaxing in the shade of a vast oak, he surveyed the calm around him. The open park was a fixture of the European scene that hadn't really survived the Atlantic crossing. Although there were many areas designated as parks in America, they were more often than not open spaces utilized for community sports or ingesting burnt meat or they were natural vistas of extreme beauty set aside as objects of wonder that could be viewed with the purchase of a ticket. There existed very few parks where the tree and its surrounding carpet of grass were the main attraction, where you could sit and do nothing and see nothing being done around you. Of course most of the European parks had begun as the front lawns of the nobility but Winston didn't care. In this age of stress and speed, the open park was not only a place to enjoy a quiet sit but a necessity for survival and Winston right now had survival very much on his mind. Avoiding Conran, who would want to discuss retreat business, and Eric Shrove, who wanted the same thing as Winston to find Mr. Smelton, was not going to be easy. Getting around the castle unassisted had seemed to be almost impossible so far and Winston wished he had spent more time identifying where Claire's hidden cameras were lurking. If he could get back to his cell without attracting any attention, the pursuit of Thomas Smelton would be that much easier. There must be another entrance into the castle, Winston reasoned, and it must be on the back curtain wall that supported the main buildings. He would start looking there and if sirens went off, what had he lost but time? He had all afternoon.

How to approach the rear of the castle and appear nonchalant and non-covert? Hands in pocket, head casually rolling this way then that, taking in the close scenery, bending to observe some natural curiosity, Winston made his way through the woods and thick underbrush that grew unchecked behind the towering wall that was the north end of the castle. Here were few windows and from what Winston could detect, no cameras bolted to the turrets. The wall had been constructed up against the hill and received very little sunlight so that the path just below the wall was sodden and cool, smelling of putrefaction and damp earth, the wall itself being slimy with moisture and lichen. Halfway along Winston found steps leading down to what looked like a cellar door, its panes dark with grime and age. First walking the full length of the wall, Winston returned to descend the steps and give the knob a turn. The door opened.

Instead of a cellar Winston found a long, dimly lit corridor that wound under the castle for some distance before coming to another set of stairs that led upward. Here a door opened into a hallway that was intersected by a second hallway. Winston took a moment to orient himself to what he already knew about the castle interior. The entrance corridor had taken two turns, a sharp left and then a right and if he wasn't totally confused, the hall directly before him would lead toward the reception area or at least to the front of the main building. To the left would be in the general direction of the library and the dining hall and to the right . . . well, he wasn't sure but if it took a left turn at some point it might take him to a spot near his room. Winston started to his right.

The hallway was obviously intended to be used by servants, for it gave no indication of castleness and other than a few mottled, hunting prints was drab, the architectural details uneventful. Winston could have been stalking the service hall of a large hotel or hospital. Instead of turning to the left as Winston had hoped, the corridor led to a large room, empty except for four closed doors. Trying all the doors, he found two locked and two open. One appeared to be a large storage closet full of cardboard boxes, all taped shut and with no markings to indicate what might be inside. The other opened onto yet another set of stairs which seemed to be the fire exit for three successive corridors of rooms identical to the one on which Winston was bedded, the third and last floor being his. He entered his hallway through a door located under the stone steps that led up to the belvedere, the very one on which Winston had met Thomas Smelton. Up to now the alarms had been quiet and Winston, starting to relax, was beginning to feel good about his adventure, that maybe he'd have some time to explore the belvedere on his own and confirm his thoughts concerning the earlier, sudden disappearance of Smelton. For when the man had left the belvedere yesterday evening, he had not gone down the steps on which Winston was now standing. Another exit had been used. Winston had made it to the third step when the door at the far end of the corridor opened and Eric Shrove bounced into the hall.

"Ohhhh, Winston. There you are. I've been all over the place looking for you. Claire said you'd passed the guard house ages ago."

"Hi Eric." Winston sat on the stairs, barely refraining from dropping his head into his hands. Eric waited until he was next to Winston before speaking again in a low voice.

"Have you been looking for Mr. Smelton?"

"Eh . . . no. Not yet."

"Oh good, then we can proceed together. I have some ideas of my own." Eric puffed out his chest.

"Swell. Look, Eric before we go off on this adventure maybe you could answer a few questions for me."

"Sure." Eric didn't appear enthusiastic about the idea.

"I'm not clear as to why you need to see Thomas Smelton. You think he's in danger?"

Eric stood staring over Winston's shoulder and up the stone stairway for a full thirty seconds.

"Eric, I'm down here."

"Sorry."

"You said out on the lawn that unless we found Smelton he'd wind up dead like Barefoot. That finding the man would save the estate from being developed. I need answers to these questions before I stick my neck out any further. Like you, I'm not a very brave man."

Eric's face went through a series of agonizing masks before he came to his decision.

"I need for you to please not tell anyone."

"Why?"

"Because if what I'm about to tell you gets out then I'll be the one to die."

Shaking his head at the thought, Eric looked on the verge of tears. What was Winston to do? What was so important around this place to warrant death penalties?

"Okay, okay. I'll keep it to myself," said Winston with his fingers mentally crossed. If for one second it put his own body in jeopardy then all promises were rescinded. Looking back down the hall, Eric made sure they were alone and leaned in even closer to Winston.

"The people that lent Justin the money to buy this place aren't very nice. In fact, they're not nice at all." Eric presented this fact to Winston as if explaining that there was no Santa. "The land was sold by Smelton under the conditions that it remain intact until he passed away."

"I knew that."

"You did?" Eric thought about that. "How did you know that?"

"I . . . eh . . . read the deed," lied Winston. "I had Conran send what I thought might be appropriate papers to New York."

"Oh. Well, then you know that as long as Smelton is alive then the property can't be sold."

"You just mentioned it."

"Oh yeah. Well . . . Justin's partners knew this but Justin said it didn't mean anything, that a good

167

lawyer could get the covenant reversed at any time."

"Can't they follow through the same way?"

"These people don't do things that way. When they hear about Justin's death, they'll expedite the situation the quickest way they know how. They have a lot of money invested."

"You mean they want to shorten Smelton's life and get on with the sale?"

Eric nodded in the affirmative.

"Great." A thought came to Winston and he gave Eric a curious look.

"Not me. Good gracious no. I couldn't hurt anyone." Eric sat on the steps next to Winston. "This whole thing is getting out of hand. Justin promised me it would go according to plan and no one would get hurt. I don't care about the money anymore. I just want to go back to Washington and forget the whole thing."

"What about your friends?"

"Them." Eric might have been talking about the ghouls from *Night of the Living Dead*. Grabbing Winston's arm, Eric whined for a glimmer of understanding. "That's why I have to find Smelton, to warn him. If he reverses the conditions of the sale, his life will no longer be in danger. He already has plenty of money, he could go anywhere and live a comfortable life and everyone would be happy."

"Would the Oblates be happy?"

Eric obviously hadn't included Conran and friends in his scenario.

"The Oblates? What do they have to do with it? They knew their time here was finite."

Wait a minute. Eric's naivete was charming but somebody connected with the retreat had a very different opinion about finiteness, thought Winston.

168

Ask Barefoot. Suddenly a light went on way in the back of Winston's brain, a dim light but an illumination all the same.

"And you think you can convince him to do this?"

Eric nodded.

"And if you can't?"

"Then I know I've tried and you're free to go to the police. How's that?"

"Well . . ." That sounded fair but Winston wasn't convinced. Now he didn't know who to trust and how come Conran had never mentioned the existence of one Thomas Smelton or of another "castle within a castle." Perhaps he shouldn't put all his eggs in one basket.

"That sounds all right but I'd like to put it off for one hour. I need to be alone and think all this out. I might even have some idea of how to reach Smelton."

"One hour? That's okay. We can meet back here." Standing, Eric took a deep breath and smiled. "I really appreciate this."

"Fine. Oh, just one question."

"Yes?"

"How come *you* don't know how to find him. I would think any of the board members would know the castle inside and out."

"Oh, that's easy. I've never been here."

"What?"

"The board meetings have always been held in Washington at Justin's request. Everyone stayed at his home."

End of conversation. Turning, Eric headed his chubby little body down the hall. At the door he paused to give a wave.

Winston needed to use a private phone and that

would not be easy at the retreat. Knowing Dace had his own line, Winston waited a few minutes before ducking back under the stairs and out the way he had entered. If he hurried he could be back in time to do some exploration on his own, but the phone call had to come first.

Chapter 20

Tying her small boat up to a cleat, Mary climbed the wooden ladder that led up to the dock. So far she was lucky. If Dutch had been around, he would have been out on his deck the minute her Evinrude had neared the boathouse, and the chance of anyone else being about was slim. Rarely did the executive branch of the retreat bother with life at the river. Even those deliverees who arrived by water were greeted at the castle. Of course Justin Barefoot had probably known this, coming to the river for a quiet moment.

Mary stood unmoving for a minute, letting the sounds around her become familiar. Should a new sound enter the landscape she wanted to make sure her senses would recognize it as such.

The *Hyorky* rocked gently as Mary scooted over the gunwale and quickly made her way forward and an inspection of the boat's two anchors. Neither one was new. Of course it meant nothing really. The new anchor could be below or in the storage area of the boathouse. Inspecting the anchors more closely, Mary saw that one had a stress crack in its casting. That would explain the purchase of a new one. If Dutch was going to use one of his anchors as a resting weight, this would have been the natural choice. It needed to be replaced anyway.

Two crows at the far end of the dock suddenly lifted into the air. Quickly, Mary hid herself on the river side of the pilot house. Scanning the path leading up to the castle, she detected a reluctant head slowly working its way toward her. Recognizing his head, she had to suppress a laugh as it bobbed up here and then there, cautiously approaching the boat-house and the *Hyorky*. She waited for the figure to slouch past her before standing and shouting.

"Yo!"

Clutching at himself, Winston almost fell.

"Bang you're dead."

"Don't do that. I have a weak body."

"I know, I've seen it."

"Thanks a lot. What are you doing here? Being a friend or a reporter?" Winston slumped over the gunwale.

"I'm not sure at the moment. I came to check on your Dutch-involvement-angle."

"What do you mean?"

"Well if Dutch had anything to do with the latest burial at sea, then he used an anchor, for that's what was wrapped around the poor slob. Seems the *Hyorky* still has its full compliment."

"I'm old friends with this one," said Winston.

"How's that?"

"I was treated to a noon cruise today. With lunch."

"Dutch gave you a cruise . . . and lunch?"

"Yeah. Hudson River nouveau. In return I got to play with the anchor."

"What's that mean?"

"Dutch was testing a new chain or something and he let me lower the anchor over the side. I may have to travel with a chiropractor from now on."

172

"A new chain?"

"Yeah. Dutch said he'd put on a new chain or something and wanted to test it."

"Sorry, I . . ." Mary stared at the anchor.

"What's going on?"

"There isn't any new chain."

"There isn't?"

"Doesn't seem to be."

"Hmmm."

"By the way, I enjoyed your approach pattern." Mary managed to smile.

"Always glad to be comic relief. It's called being careful. People get murdered around this place, remember. I was going to borrow Dutch's phone if he was home . . . and what's with the chain?"

"I don't know. Wait on the dock for me, will you? I want to check for something below." Mary disappeared into the salon. Sitting on the deck, Winston watched the boats out on the river. Was it possible that Conran had arranged for Dutch to keep him away from the castle for a few hours. And if so, why?

"I want to check in the storage area. I'll just be a second." Mary jumped past him onto the dock.

"What are you looking for?"

"I'm not sure. Go on into Dutch's, I'll be right there."

Dutch's apartment looked like the inside of a well stocked rod and tackle store. A large, glass topped table exhibited fishing lures and on the walls were hung numerous rods of varying shapes and sizes along with an assortment of river memorabilia. Winston stopped to scrutinize a photograph of a paddle steamer.

"Nice collection of stuff, hey?" said Mary coming into the apartment.

"I feel I should buy something."

"You'd have a hard time. Most of these lures and poles are antiques. These flies here were tied by Dutch himself."

"To what? Torture?"

"Cute. It takes great skill to do this. There's the phone."

"I don't need it now."

"How's that?"

"I was going to call you and arrange for a meeting later." Winston poked a stuffed fish. "You free later?"

Mary plopped into a chair.

"Depends on what you have in mind, big boy."

"Ohhh . . . an Italian dinner on Mott Street *in* New York City followed by years of unbounded happiness."

"How about drinks on the deck around eleven and one more night swim? Don't look so glum. You make me very happy but I'm afraid it's one boom-boom at a time for this woman."

"Boom-boom?"

"I have a support group meeting tonight. Doesn't usually get out 'til ten . . . ten-thirty."

"Is this a consciousness raising thing or do you actually hold something up?"

Mary stopped herself from laughing and shook her head.

"Why do I laugh at your crap? It's a group of women with different problems. We talk and help each other, or try to. It's honest and up front and we don't have to wear monk robes or flagellate ourselves with health food."

"Sorry. Humor is my way of handling unwarranted anxiety."

Mary held her hand up for Winston to hold.

"No, I'm sorry. I'm feeling a little fragile and it's

upsetting. It's a feeling I'm not used to."

Winston sat in the other chair.

"Listen babe, I've just had a flash on this castle situation. Want to hear it?"

"Sure." Mary perked up.

"Off-the-record? For a couple of days." Winston had a passing image of Captain Sweetman sitting opposite him.

Mary reluctantly shook her head in agreement.

"Up until this afternoon I thought there were two opposing camps here: the Washington group and the Buddingville group."

"The sellers and the keepers?"

"Right. At first I wasn't exactly clear on who belonged to what camp but now, except for Melody Pinklingill who may be a loose cannon, I think the sides are pretty well delineated. Conran and Shea versus Barefoot and Shrove."

"Did the Conran camp eliminate a member of the opposing camp?"

"Well, that's just it. I don't think either Conran or Cynthia Shea killed anyone. I can't prove they didn't, it's just a hunch. But in both cases I think these people are fronts for larger interests and it's those larger interests that are capable of doing anything."

"What larger interests?"

"Eric Shrove told me that Barefoot used investors' money to buy the majority interest in the Smelton estate and that these investors were not very nice guys *and* that these not very nice guys were pushing to get their investment resolved."

"So Barefoot was pushing for a sale."

"That's right. But according to the deed he *can't* sell it for included in the selling contract was a rider that stated that until the seller had died the property could not be sold."

"Wait a minute. The seller being Thomas Smelton."

"Uh huh."

Mary was on her feet.

"I knew it! Last night when you mentioned meeting Bozo the Crazy I had a feeling it might be Smelton. I could never get Dutch to 'fess up but there's always been a rumor circulating that Smelton never left the area after the sale and that actually he was still at the castle. Of course nobody could ever substantiate the damn thing. What a story!"

"Off-the-record, remember?"

"For a couple of days. Remember?"

"Okay but I have first shot at the guy."

"What do you mean?"

"Eric Shrove thinks these bad guys are going to hurry the sale of the castle by sending someone up here to off the poor old man. He wants me to find and warn him."

"What does Shrove care?"

"Claims he's fed up with the whole thing and just wants to go home and live a quiet *safe* life."

"I wouldn't trust Shrove."

"He's a fat, little accountant afraid of his own shadow. I think he's telling the truth."

"Maybe." Mary couldn't stand still. "What do you know? The Thomas Smelton factor."

"That's it. So suddenly we have these warring camps with a third party stuck in the middle."

"A third party that one group would like to keep around as security and the other group . . . bingo."

"More fish food."

"Bozo the Crazy has put himself in a dangerous position." Mary sat back down.

"Yeah, and I wonder if he's aware of his position."

"Sounds like he's not aware of too much."

"Maybe not but he sure made the right move to insure that the castle and he stayed together until the very end."

"That's true. Crazy like a fox. So why's it so hard to find him. There's only so many doors in the place."

"Well this is where it gets a little stranger. Seems there's a 'castle within the castle' whatever that means."

"Secret rooms?"

"Probably something like that. I think there may be a series of hidden passageways that crisscross the castle. Smelton lives in them. Possibly."

"The Hidden Castle. I love it. Come on, let's go find the guy."

"Hold it, hold it. We're forgetting something." Winston peeked into Dutch's refrigerator.

"What? We forgot to look in the fridge?"

"Two beers and a bag of coffee beans. At least I keep a jar of mayonnaise in mine."

"What did we forget, damn it?"

"Who do Conran and Cynthia front for?"

Mary stopped pacing.

"If they do."

"Well somebody thought something was important enough to bump off Barefoot and then there's this mystery man wrapped around an anchor. An anchor that may have started its life in this very boathouse."

"We don't know that yet and Barefoot *may* have been killed by those not very nice guys I've been hearing about."

"Possible, but I don't think so. As far as the bad guys knew, everything was going according to plan. I can't imagine Barefoot mentioned Thomas Smelton to his investors."

"So who *do* they front for?"

"I have no idea. The only odd behavior I've noticed around this place is the Oblates themselves."

Winston and Mary sat looking at one another.

"What could a retreat front for?" asked Mary.

"I don't know but . . ."

"But what?"

"That's where you come in," Winston pointed out.

"Me?"

"Maybe you could find out who the anchor man was. Don't reporters have sources for that sort of info? I bet that once we know who he is, we have a major piece of the puzzle."

"Or a bigger mystery."

"Either way it's a great scoop, eh?"

"You bet and it just so happens that that's what I'm doing at this support group meeting tonight."

Mary followed Winston into the other room of the apartment.

"How's that?"

"My informant with the police is one of the group and she tells me everything. I called her today and asked her to bring me the lowdown on this guy tonight."

Affecting an English accent, Winston gave Dutch's bed a probe with an index finger.

"I say . . . might this be a boom-boom room?"

"Forget it, city slicker." Mary backed into the front room. "How could you be thinking about sex at a time like this? There's exciting work to do."

"I'm a product of my times. Don't you know . . . look at a movie, read a book, watch the tube: sex and violence go hand in hand. Don't you read your own paper?"

"Listen lover . . ." Mary wrapped her arms around Winston's waist. ". . . a time for everything. Tonight under the stars when we've tucked this mystery in bed for the evening, we'll take another swim, lie on the raft, and search the heavens for Orion's belt or something . . ."

"Let's keep old boyfriends out of this, okay? I'm . . ."

The slam of the screen door was like a bullet passing between them.

"Dutch!"

Jumping back from Winston, Mary immediately felt foolish. Dutch didn't care who she held on to, his concerns lay elsewhere. Dutch held her gaze for a full ten seconds before the razor grin began its slow line across his face.

"Orion's belt won't be up 'til after midnight. Raft could get mighty cold by then," mused Dace.

"I'm sorry, Dutch. I know you don't like people in here when you're not around but we needed to use the phone."

"A safe harbor," offered Winston.

"Don't count on that, Cap." Dutch's grin faded. "Have you made your call?"

"Sure, Dutch." Mary brought Dutch's focus back to her. "I have a question."

"Shoot."

"How does somebody find Thomas Smelton? And don't bullshit me. I know he's here somewhere."

Dutch spent a moment observing the two faces before him, his eyes settling on one and then the other. Mary knew he wouldn't lie but he could be inventively evasive.

"I don't know."

"But you admit he's here somewhere."

"I've never seen him. I seem to recall hearing some place that he hated boats. Just looking at one made him seasick."

Mary grinned. Smelton was here all right but he never came to the boathouse. Probably never left the castle. Mary knew she shouldn't ask this next question but the reporter in her was too strong.

"Winston thinks the retreat is a front for something else. Is that true?"

Dutch surprised her by laughing.

"Mr. Wyc can think anything he wants. You're talking to the wrong person, Mary. You and your friend should try the castle crowd. Answering questions is what they do."

"How about anchors?" asked Mary. "I was told there was a new one around somewhere but I can't seem to find it."

"What the hell you been doing?" Dutch was no longer amused.

"I was down talking to Everett . . ." Mary shrugged.

"Quite the reporter, aren't we? This is your old pal Dutch, remember?"

Brushing past them, Dutch picked up a small overnight bag lying next to the refrigerator. Hesitating at the door, he glanced quickly at Winston before turning his clouded expression toward Mary.

"Forget about it, Mary." Dutch's voice was barely audible. "Lock up when you leave."

Slamming the door, Dutch's descending tread fell silent on the stone steps outside.

"I've never seen Dutch so mad," said Mary.

"That stuff about the anchor got to him. What was that all about?"

"I'll explain later. I don't feel so great."

From a window above the sink, Winston could see Dutch and his bag board the *Hyorky*. Was the man taking a trip?

"After the cruise this morning, Dutch warned me not to hang around. I'm still not sure why. He seemed to become upset over a nun sitting near the riverbank. I don't think I was supposed to have seen her."

"A nun? What was she doing?"

"Having a smoke."

"A smoke?"

"And watching the river go by as far as I could see. Nothing more, nothing less."

The deep bark of the *Hyorky* interrupted their silence. Mary moved quickly out onto the deck. Winston joined her at the parapet wall as the boat inched slowly away from the dock.

"Wonder where he's off to?" asked Winston.

"He's angry. Probably going to let off steam. Winston . . ." Mary leaned into Winston's arm. "When does one stop being a reporter?"

"You found something out and Dutch *is* involved, isn't he?"

"You were right. Whatever's going on here, Dutch has a part in it." Mary was surprised at how despondent her voice sounded.

"Don't take it so hard. I think the death of Barefoot has changed Dutch's involvement with this thing. Whatever it is he won't be part of it much longer. I think he's really worried about you."

"Maybe. You going to help Shrove find Smelton?"

"Not quite yet. You want to come?"

"No, I have to get my boat back to the cottage and get ready for tonight."

Surprising herself yet again, Mary leaned into Winston, placing her head on his chest and holding him.

"I'll see you later, okay? Don't get yourself hurt."

"Maybe I'll invite old Tom over for pizza tonight."

"You do that, you silly bastard."

Winston watched as Mary's boat putted out into

the river and turned the corner before he moved down the shoreline. Stopping about a hundred yards from the boathouse, he began searching the ground for something. Ten minutes passed before he found what he was looking for. Winston was no forensic expert but he would swear that the cigarette stub he held was of the same kind that he had seen in the room above the library. Non-filtered and fatter than an American cigarette. Winston turned it slowly in his fingers. There was no brand name and its odor was strong, foreign. Whoever had been sitting on the bank earlier that day enjoying a smoke had either traveled lately or had exotic smoking habits. They also had definitely been sitting in that room just before Winston entered it. Winston looked up at the sky. Evening was approaching quickly, the sun having reached the hills behind him, sending long shadows out into the Hudson River.

Chapter 21

Winston was amazed. He had gone straight from the river and into the castle through the portico doors, through the conservatory, down several hallways and up the flight of stairs to his room and had not run into a single person. If he was lucky, the rest of the evening would be more of the same. Had he been anxious about roaming the castle before, Winston felt particularly uneasy now wondering if Thomas Smelton was peering at him from some peephole. Every hollow in the cornice, every irregularity in the wall blinked at him as he made his way to his cell which, he was delighted to see, appeared as he remembered: dull and uninviting. Sitting on the cot, Winston went over in his mind once again the evening's labor. Should his thoughts concerning the stairs to the belvedere prove wrong, then he knew of one other place where he might gain access to the secret world of Mr. Smelton.

Opening his briefcase, Winston took out a Swiss Army knife and a pen sized flashlight that he always carried with him. These tools were invaluable when dating old houses or examining documents in the dark basements of government buildings. The knife's various instruments were all one needed to scrape or probe one's way back to the original house waiting below the years of grime. Or as another historian might say, patina. Winston had used the corkscrew to twist around a cut nail and remove it from soft wood. Nails which were used to join subflooring or sheathing or even interior moldings could almost always be used to help date a building. Handmade nails, rectangular and hammered to a point, almost always predate eighteen hundred. Cut nails, made rectangular and tapered by a machine, might have handmade heads which show a vice pinch just below the hammered head; these date from about seventeen ninety until eighteen twenty-five. Or, they could be the later machine-headed cut nails which would have no pinch, appear identical, and date from around eighteen twenty-five to eighteen ninety. After that time, wire nails replaced cut nails for finish application. The awl could produce an inconspicuous hole in which Winston could shine the small flashlight and see if the lath behind the plaster was riven or machine made. The can opener was excellent for scraping away layers of paint or wallpaper without leaving a wide swath. The blade could be slipped easily into that hairline fracture in the wainscotting or the butt joint in the walnut paneling to feel what, if anything, existed beneath or behind.

A wooden rule completed Winston's exploration tools. He preferred it over a tape measure, for when extended to full length it could be held out straight without bending. Also, it provided a metal extension for measuring accurately inside dimensions.

Laying these instruments on the cot, Winston stood and removed his sport coat and put on his navy blue sweater that he had brought in case the country proved to be cold. For Winston, any place fifty miles north of New York City bordered on the Hudson Bay. Wasn't that why they called it the Hudson River? Winston felt a night watch cap and charcoal under the eyes might be appropriate but decided not to carry the fantasy too far. As nutty as the residents seemed, they would probably object to his walking around impersonating a second-story burglar. Glancing around at the stone walls of his cell, Winston wondered if his little preparation was being observed. Until he was doing the peeping, he was not going to be able to relax. Sighing deeply, Winston completed his preparation with a silent prayer to the patron saint of architecture who, oddly enough, was St. Thomas.

The hallway appeared clear. Winston was surprised that Eric Shrove hadn't made an appearance for the allotted delay of one hour had passed some time ago. Was the man lurking? Winston could see no appropriately chubby shadows. Of course, four other doors stood between his and the stairs. A light foot was needed.

At the steps, Winston hesitated and listened. The tomb-like silence of the hall remained as such. Satisfied that he was alone, Winston climbed the stairs to the belvedere. The width of the steps became narrower after each landing and beyond the third very narrow, measuring only twenty-eight inches. Not enough room for two people to pass. Here the steps spiraled up in a wide arc as if to the top of a turret. Winston remembered reading somewhere that all tower stairs in old castles were fashioned to ascend clockwise because it made it difficult for a right-handed enemy climbing the stairs to swing his

185

sword. If the tower at this point was as wide as at the bottom, and from outside that seemed to be the case, then there was plenty of room in the center of the spiral arc to hide another set of stairs, particularly if they followed the same curve. What Winston had to do was find the entrance and he was sure that that would be at the top just as you entered to go in or come down. A person leaving the belvedere was immediately confronted with the stairs leading down and wouldn't spend any time exploring the stone wall to his left against which the door rested. Coming from below, you would waste little time opening the door, for there was no landing and the narrow space was uncomfortable. Winston wondered how many of the retreat guests ever actually climbed the steps to enjoy the view. The encouraged focus seemed to be more inward.

Winston inspected the stone wall behind where the entrance door to the belvedere swung open. A vertical row of coin-shaped bezants, looking very much like push buttons, formed an arch over the passageway exactly at the point where the door met the wall. Winston began manipulating the raised bezants.

"You're late, Winston."

Eric Shrove stood suddenly in the doorway, his small bulk blocking the sunlight. Surprised, Winston grabbed at the stones, trying to keep from falling down the stairs.

"Sorry. Did I give you a fright?" Eric's expression bordered on a smirk.

Containing himself, Winston considered his options: backwards down the steps or headlong over the rail. With a running start he could probably reach the parking lot. Either stunt should produce the right amount of pain.

"I've been watching you down at the boat-house . . ." Eric nodded toward the mounted binoculars. ". . . and I must say you've been very busy."

"I had an appointment." Winston was beginning to be irked by this doughboy. "It ran late."

"Talking to reporters?"

"Talking to a friend."

"I think the time would be better spent trying to find Mr. Smelton."

"Oh yeah? You want to find Thomas Smelton, Eric, you go right ahead. I'm going to enjoy the view for a while."

For a split second, Shrove's face went thin, the skin sucked tight by some inner tension. Whether fright or anger, Winston couldn't be sure because just as quickly, the anguish vanished. Winston had a sudden feeling that maybe he wasn't dealing with just a chubby, little accountant who meant well and could be trusted. The man's eyes had been damned scary.

"Sorry. Didn't mean to step on any toes." Eric assumed his schoolboy pose. "I thought you had forgotten me."

"Forget you, Eric? Impossible." Winston closed his eyes and counted to six. "Let's forget it. I'm the one who should apologize. I think the murder is taking its toll on my social graces."

Reddening, Eric shrugged.

"That's okay. You know, I had this really strange thought, Winston. What if Mr. Smelton knew who the murderer was? Or maybe he could give us some valuable clue and we could solve the crime. We'd be heroes."

Winston had to think about this one for a minute. The man seemed real, his enthusiasm genuine, his naivete still intact. Then where had the Angel of Death eyes come from? Was Eric Shrove really Dr. Shrove and Mr. Hyde? Winston was sure of one thing, he didn't need a fellow explorer at this point and certainly not "Doughboy of the Damned." Perhaps some innocent wall tapping in the conservatory or a candle lit search of the basement passageway could occupy his portly pal. They could split up. Eric could run his stubby fingers around the raised paneling in the library feeling for hidden releases, that would take some time, while Winston hustled back to the belvedere.

"Look Eric, I have an idea. Why don't we go down to the . . ."

"Yoo hoo! Mr. Wyc! Over here!"

Turning their heads as one, Winston and Eric found Conran and Cynthia Shea waving at them from the other belvedere which rose equidistant from the main entrance on the other end of the castle.

"Stay there, we'll come over," shouted Conran. The two disappeared instantly.

"Damn," muttered Winston.

"Double damn." Whispering, Eric leaned in toward Winston. "Now we can't look for Smelton." Eric's statement was almost a question.

Placing his finger to his mouth, Winston whispered back. "Not now I'm afraid. We should keep this project to ourselves."

Giggling, Eric went to the door to listen for Conran and Cynthia. Winston peered out over the estate grounds and down to the Hudson. The *Hyorky* was visible up the river. It had traveled far enough so that Winston couldn't tell whether it was still moving or not. Although the sun wouldn't actually set for another two hours, it had passed beyond the hill behind the castle, and the lawn lay in shadow up to the point where it fell away to the river. Staring at the sun speckled water, Winston felt as if he was trapped in a land of darkness. A tear in time had revealed another land, a land of brightness and warmth that lay forever beyond his reach. You can't get there from here, mister.

"They're coming."

Hurrying back to the railing, Eric arranged himself in as nonchalant a pose as he was able. In spite of himself, Winston had to smile for Eric looked like Peter Lorre auditioning for the role of Camille, needing only a rose to complete the picture. A series of grunts and curses preceded Conran's explosion onto the floor. The man hit the deck like a champagne cork pulled from a bottle; Cynthia Shea tumbling behind, caught in the vacuum produced by Conran's too wide girth being contained by the hollow passageway. Settling against a support post, Conran took a moment to catch his breath and inspect his cowl for stone rubbings.

"Good afternoon, Ms. Shea." Winston watched as Cynthia recomposed herself. A tug here, a toss of the head there and the woman looked as sensible as ever. She managed a forced smile in Winston's direction.

"I had forgotten how narrow the damned stairway was on this side." Conran gave the stairwell opening a look of loathing, his mind already on the descent. "Perhaps I shall leave by crane. What do you think? A series of pulleys, a long, strong rope and there you have it, or rather, me, settled unto the grass below." Conran chuckled at his suggestion, his mood suddenly reversed. Winston looked over the railing in search of grass. "And Eric. Enjoying the view." Eric had moved as far away from Conran as he could get on the belvedere which Winston couldn't help but notice was getting uncomfortably crowded.

"The view is stunning, Michael. You can see a lot from up here."

"That you can, Eric. That you can."

"How has your day been, Mr. Wyc? Any new thoughts concerning the retreat?" Cynthia lingered near the door. Winston had the feeling she was afraid of heights.

"I find the castle and the grounds very . . . interesting. Whether or not it's suitable for historic designation I can't be sure at the moment. Got any friends in Washington?"

"What's that supposed to mean?" Cynthia almost looked in Conran's direction.

"I simply mean that sometimes friends in high places can do more than twenty reams of well thought out paperwork. That's all."

"Of course that's what you meant and actually we do have a few strings we might be able to pull in the administration. You think that might be necessary?" said Conran.

"I don't know. Like I said before, if I were you I'd start with the local government or planning board. They could prove to be more of a help and quickly."

"You did mention that."

"You still want to go through with the application?" asked Winston incredulously.

"Well . . ." Conran glanced over at Eric. "It still has to be discussed by the board. Maybe we could write up a menu of options and the board could start from there. Your suggestions would be appreciated. Don't you think, Cynthia?"

"Of course, Michael."

Smiling tenderly upon the gathering, Conran

suddenly turned to the railing and, lifting his arms, intoned to the lawn and river below:

> "In the greenest of our valleys
>   By good angels tenanted,
> Once a fair and stately palace—
>   Radiant palace—reared its head.
> In the monarch Thought's dominion—
>   It stood there!
> Never seraph spread a pinion
>   Over fabric half so fair!
>
> Wanderers in that happy valley,
>   Through two luminous windows, saw
> Spirits moving musically,
>   To a lute's well-tunèd law,
> Round about a throne where, sitting,
>   Porphyrogene!

Lowering his arms, Conran stopped reciting, his face crinkled into a bemused question mark.

"Porphyrogene? Can you believe that word? Only Poe could use a word like that or for that matter, even know what it meant. It always stops me cold."

"What's it mean?" asked Eric in his smallest voice.

"Who the hell knows?" boomed Conran. "Porphyrogene. Porphyrogene. Cracks me up."

"Is there something you wanted to talk about?" asked Winston.

"Well . . ." Conran looked at Cynthia.

"Actually, Michael and I wanted to talk to Eric. Board business." Cynthia's head bobbed up and down in agreement with herself.

"Privately?" asked Winston.

"If it's not too boring of us, Winston. You understand." Conran eyed Eric as he might a Tofu Supreme.

"No, no. Don't let me interfere. I could use an hour in my room jotting down a few notes."

Winston bolted for the door.

"Just a minute, Mr. Wyc." Cynthia raised her hand. "Are you planning to stay another night?"

"I think so . . . but with friends again."

"Ahhh . . . well, could I knock on your door later? After this board business?"

Winston hesitated. In actuality, an exploration of the room above the library was his destination, not his room.

"I'll take only a second of your time."

"That would be fine. If for some reason I'm not there, try the library."

"I will." Cynthia's smile was warm and friendly. It looked oddly out of sync with the rest of her face.

Giving a quick glance at the wall behind the door, Winston was down the stairwell. Further inspection of the wall would have to wait. Right now Winston probably had the next thirty minutes to himself and he wasn't going to waste it. Cynthia could catch up with him later.

Passing through the reception area, Winston met Sister Kerry coming from the opposite hallway; her small, scrubbed face full of immured sanctity.

"Good evening, Mr. Wyc."

"Good evening, Sister. Coming to work?"

"I am. Do we have the pleasure of your company for one more night?"

"For only another hour or two, I'm afraid."

Sister Kerry smiled. Winston had spent most of his youth being taught by nuns and had early in his school life divided them into either Beamers or

Frowners. These categories were broken down even further. Beamers could be Beamers Blissed or Beamers Bright, the former using their beautific smiles to hide their confusion about life, and the latter whose eyes were full of knowing and could be used as augurs to tap a young boy's secrets. Frowners were either Fussy or Furious, no explanations needed. Sister Kerry was a Beamer Bright.

"Eh . . . could I ask you a question, Sister?"

"Certainly."

"What order do you belong to?" The smile didn't actually fade but Winston could discern a loosening of the smile muscles. "I ask because my aunt is a nun and I didn't know if maybe you and she had met or were of the same order."

"Oh. Well there's many nuns."

"True. My aunt is down in the Bronx. Sisters of Tender Mercies."

"Of course, a very active convent in the community. I've heard of them. Myself, I took my vows with a small Jesuit order in Maryland, The Sisters of St. Brendan. I doubt if your aunt has ever heard of it."

"Probably not. Are all the nuns here of the same order?"

"Yes. I must get to work, Mr. Wyc. It's not fair to keep Claire after her time."

With that, Sister Kerry nodded and passed on into the office. Maryland was right next to Washington. Winston wondered if The Sisters of St. Brendan were recruited at the same time as Justin Barefoot or if Conran and the Sisters went back even further. Captain Sweetman might want to look up that information. Hurrying down the corridor and through the conservatory, Winston ran smack into Melody Pinklingill and the Engine.

"Well, well, if it isn't our historian. Just returning, Mr. Wyc, or have we not left yet?"

Melody Pinklingill was all aglow this evening in a dress of bright, blue forget-me-nots on a Nile green background, a baby blue shawl about her shoulders and a string of silver balls around her neck. A hint of lipstick and matching rouge added to the bloom. Winston thought she appeared quite pleased with herself, her eyes twinkly, her mouth pursed into a self-satisfied grin. The Engine was pinched into her usual dark habit.

"Yes, I'm still hanging about, but not for much longer. Are you going out tonight?" Winston nodded to Sister Mary who looked straight through him.

"I am out, aren't I?" said Miss Pinklingill.

"That's true, but you look special this evening. I thought that maybe you had something special in mind."

Taking a moment to answer, Miss Pinklingill rested her head back and peered into what could only have been the future. Obviously she enjoyed what she saw.

"I've had a good day, Mr. Wyc, the kind of day that lifts the spirits. It's difficult to remain at home when one feels lifted."

"I see. Are you staying for dinner?"

"Dinner? Good gracious no, why would I do that?"

Winston could see where that might be unlifting. No need to let a plate of Tempeh Royale or for that matter, the recent murder of a friend, ruin one's day.

"Actually I've been told by Cynthia that we have a board meeting at six-thirty. In the conference room." Miss Pinklingill checked her watch.

"The conference room?"

"Yes, it's a room off the reception area small enough so that everyone has to listen to each other or at least pretend to. Also it's private."

This last sentence was delivered more to Sister Mary than to Winston who wondered if this conference room was one of the few spaces sealed off from the prying ears of one Thomas Smelton. Winston checked his watch.

"It should seem larger now," said Winston.

"I . . ." Miss Pinklingill's grin broadened ever so slightly as she realized what Winston meant. "Very naughty, Mr. Wyc. But point well taken. Hopefully we'll talk again before your departure. Come, Mary."

Winston waited until Miss Pinklingill and the Engine were nearly through the conservatory before entering the library. Nothing had changed since the previous morning. Circling the room, Winston let the events of that meeting run slowly through his mind: the seating arrangement, what had been said up to the argument, whether anyone had actually listened to him, the noises he had heard and people he had seen directly afterward. Everyone was accounted for except Claire who might have left the library the same time as Conran and Winston would not have seen her. As far as Winston could remember, by the time he had spotted Barefoot out on the lawn everyone except Conran had dispersed in directions away from the boathouse. But then Winston had seen Conran only moments prior to the murder and unless the man was much faster than he looked, Conran could not have been the murderer. So where did that leave us? There must have been an accomplice, reasoned Winston, and the only person to leave the library before the meeting adjourned was Sister Mary Crosse. Winston had seen her. Could she have delivered a message to someone smoking in the room above? A smoking nun? And if someone had snuck out of the castle, who might have seen them? Perhaps Thomas Smelton?

Pacing off the width of the room, Winston reentered the hall and seeing no one, bounded up the stairs and past the chain that divided public from private. As he turned the corner, Winston thought he heard a door click shut down the hall before him. He waited. After counting to twenty-five, he started down the hall, stopping at each door, listening for movement or sound, but heard nothing. He knocked softly on the door to the room above the library and still hearing nothing, opened the door carefully. This time the room was really empty. Gone were all of the personal belongings Winston had seen previously, and except for a single nun's habit that hung on a hook in the closet, the room was bare. Whoever had been using the room had either left or had moved to other quarters. Winston had a feeling that the person was probably no longer on the premises.

Placing one foot directly in front of the other, Winston paced off the width of the room. Roughly sixteen feet. It was five feet narrower than the library below. This was a good start but Winston would have to get into the room next to it to know if he had stumbled onto anything. Out in the hall, he paced off the distance from the end wall to the casing of the door on the other room. Twenty two feet exactly. Winston placed his ear against the door and concentrated on the noises within. Cautiously, he turned the knob. The door was locked. Dropping to his knees, Winston tried peering under the door to see if the adjacent wall could be seen, but the room was dark and offered no details. Although not stone, the walls

here were plaster and thick and finding the whereabouts of the wall by rapping would be difficult if
not noisy. Winston returned to the end room. If there
was a hidden passageway between the two rooms
then obviously it was either from this side or the
other. Starting with the closet, Winston began a
meticulous inspection of the wall. All mouldings
were tight and there seemed to be no seams in the
plaster. Taking out his Swiss Army knife, Winston
picked a section near the floor of the closet and
began to probe the wall. By shining his flashlight
through a small hole, Winston could see if a passageway did indeed exist. If that turned out to be the case,
then he could renew his efforts. Winston shut off his
penlight. Someone had entered the room. The hard
heels on the oak floor were solid and they had
stopped halfway across the room. Winston held his
breath and listened. How was he to explain being on
his hands and knees drilling a little hole at the base of
a closet? Looking for his favorite coat hanger
probably wouldn't work. Whoever was standing in
the room hadn't moved in thirty seconds and
Winston wondered if they had sat down and were
waiting for someone or were they listening for him.
Was this person the killer? Inching himself to a
standing position, Winston was playing with the
idea of sneaking a look when the person did move,
their footfalls heading in the direction of the
windows. Hearing his chance, Winston peered from
around the door jamb. Leaning into the deep
windowsill was a nun, a large nun. Not so tall but
wide, her dark habit filling the opening. A nun was
not normally someone to fear, but something about
this one—the insolence of the heavy shoulders, the
deliberateness of the thickset fingers as they played

with the window curtains—made Winston hold back. Next to the nun was a black traveling bag, the soft canvas type with a hard bottom and long shoulder strap. Light from the outside was fading quickly, and as the room darkened, Winston wondered if he was going to spend the evening in the closet or if he should swallow his fear and bluff his way out of the room. Could there be an escape other than the elusive secret passageway? An idea came to him. An idea that comes only to people trapped in small spaces who have had very little sleep. Carefully, very carefully, he slipped the nun's habit off its hook and over his head. It must have been made for Sister Mary Crosse, for it fit him easily in width if not in length, stopping just short of his knees. A mini habit. Collecting himself, Winston exited the closet as quietly as possible, his hands clasped beatifically before him, surprised at how a piece of clothing could give him such a sense of virtue. The door knob was but inches away when the voice stopped him.

"Who the hell are you?"

"Excuse me."

This nun's voice had a decidedly male resonance to it.

"You're no nun," stammered Winston.

"And no virgin either, mate. Who are you?"

"Sister . . . eh . . . Winny," Winston sputtered.

The two un-nuns stared at each other across the darkening room, one probably very comfortable with their god, the other desperately in need of one.

"Sister Winny?"

Sensing a breakdown in sisterly trust, Winston leaped at the door, jerked it open and bolted down the hall. Arriving breathless at the head of the staircase, he found Cynthia Shea ascending the stairs toward him, her expression suddenly matching his as one of surprise and confusion.

"Winston, is that you? What in the world is going on?"

"I'm not sure. Actually, I'm . . ."

Coming quickly around the corner, the masculine nun slowed upon seeing Cynthia and stopped altogether when Cynthia raised her hand for him to halt. Winston looked from one to the other and then quickly back to the nun. The Sisters of St. Brendan were certainly an odd order, he thought. Along with the induction of men they allowed the carrying of guns.

"What in the hell are you doing?" Cynthia spoke harshly to the nun.

"I ran into this girlie-man hiding in my room. What was I supposed to do? Invite'm for a cuppa?" the brawny nun barked.

"Girlie-man? Look pa . . ."

"Listen Winston. I'm sorry you had to find our friend here but I can explain everything. If you'd come with us please."

If Cynthia had used the word "me" instead of "us," Winston might have stumbled along behind her, but any initiative that involved a nun with a gun was out of the question. Winston bolted once again, this time for the door to the hallway with the peepholes.

"Shoot the bastard." Cynthia Shea didn't mince words. Wasting no time in closing the door behind him, Winston hesitated only long enough to get his bearings. Then using the slight illumination coming through the peepholes, he made his way to the end of the narrow hall and through yet another door. This one closed just as the one at the other end opened. Winston could hear Cynthia screaming something about leaving the damn habit on and getting the prick. No talk of destination now. Winston found himself tearing down another dimly lit hallway wondering why he couldn't keep his nose out of where it didn't belong.

The corridor took an abrupt right and then a left. Winston realized he had no idea where he was other than somewhere in the bowels of the castle. He had lost all sense of north and south. Footsteps could be heard coming hurriedly down the hall behind him. The corridor came to a split, one way lit, the other not. Holding his side, Winston peered into the dark passageway. What the hell. Moving cautiously down the unlit hallway, Winston felt along the smooth stone and prayed for a door. Behind him his pursuers could be seen standing at the division in the hall peering down the lit passageway and then the dark. Cynthia motioned for the nun to go into the dark passage and she took off toward the lit. Panicked, Winston moved faster. His hand fell upon a wooden panel, the raised panel of a door. Dropping his arm to doorknob height, his hand closed around the flat, vertical handle of a Norfolk thumb latch. Easing himself through the door, Winston entered another dark space. Carefully returning the latch to its cradle, he quickly dug into his pocket for his flashlight. Its beam revealed a small room with a door on the other side opposite the one he had just come through. Passing through this door, Winston stumbled into the reception area and found himself confronting the amazed faces of Michael Conran and Eric Shrove.

"Winston. What a pleasant surprise." Conran seemed genuinely happy to see him. "Exploring, are we?"

Winston stared into the dark room behind him and

closing the door, hurried along to where the other men stood gawking at him. How long before his nun friend arrived, he couldn't be sure, but it wouldn't be long enough.

"Having a look around, yes. Yes, indeed," said Winston catching his breath.

"Are you okay?" asked Eric.

"Sure, I'm fine." Winston shrugged.

"Wonderful edifice, heh. Makes one want to don the armor and . . ."

"I'm sorry, Michael, I'd love to talk but I have to get to my room immediately. Something's come up."

"Ohhh, nothing serious I hope?" Conran's face took on a guarded look.

Winston shook his head no and, trying not to run, moved toward the door to his stairway. Only when halfway up the stairs did he wonder why he hadn't gone for the exit. As Winston reached his floor, he could hear a loud commotion below him. People seemed to be shouting and one of the voices was most certainly Cynthia Shea's. Grabbing his briefcase from his room, Winston headed down the hall to the back stairs and what he knew to be the underground tunnel out of the castle. Stopping at the end of the hall, he looked up the spiral stairs that curved up to the belvedere. One more try. Why not, he thought. They'd never look on the belvedere for him. Not for a while anyway.

Winston shook his head as he ascended the stairs upward. This need to find the secret passageway to Thomas Smelton was becoming an obsession and a dangerous one. These people must have killed Barefoot and at this point would probably not hesitate killing him. Winston knew too much but what he knew he wasn't sure and at the moment he wasn't going to take the time to figure it out. He *was* sure that the entrance to Smelton's other castle was at the top of these stairs and that it led to a refuge of a kind. He hoped.

Reaching the door out to the belvedere, Winston took a moment to gulp down some night air. A short distance on the other side of the trees, Mary "boom boom" Bartlett would soon be sitting down in her cottage wondering where the hell he might be. Where in the hell did he find them?

Running his hands over the raised bezants that ran up the wall, Winston discovered a loose one at shoulder height. He pushed it. Nothing happened. Footsteps could be heard in the hallway below him. Someone was searching rooms. Winston tried turning the coin-shaped stone but it wouldn't move. Taking out his penlight, Winston decided to risk a light being seen. Slowly he shone the beam on each bezant and then each stone. They all looked and felt solidly in place. Was he looking for the wrong thing? Running his eyes up and down the wall, his attention rested on a small but elaborate hook protruding from the wall at ankle height that could be used to hold the exit door open—except there was no corresponding catch on the door. Winston pulled and pushed the hook. Nothing. He twisted it. A bezant popped out just above his head. Standing, Winston gave the stone a turn. Silently, a narrow door of stone opened before him. Winston slid sideways onto a dark landing. Going back out onto the stairs, Winston closed the secret door and examined the wall for seams. A v-shaped reveal that highlighted the design ran on either side of the bezant ornamentation. The reveal on the right was actually a seam but undetectable in the way the light fell across the wall. Even in daylight the seam would remain hidden. Winston could hear someone at the bottom of the stairs. Once again he twisted the hook and once again the stone popped out. Like magic, Winston thought, as he slid again through the wall and closed the secret entry behind him. A bolt clicked softly into place. Using his flashlight, Winston followed the darkened stairs downward back into the center of the castle. Calculating the distance as he went, he figured he had descended nearly three floors when he came upon an open door. Peering cautiously around the door, Winston found himself staring straight into the face of the man he had met on the belvedere his first day at the retreat.

"My goodness," said the man backing up. "My goodness . . . my goodness . . ."

Almost as shocked as the old man, Winston took a second to still his pounding heart. The gentleman finally came to rest against a table, his hands up before him, his eyes wide with fright.

"It's okay. I'm a friend." Winston dared not move.

"How could that be? We've never been introduced. Have we?"

"We met on the belvedere." Could that have been yesterday.

"Ohhh . . . yes. Did we?"

The two men stared at one another. Thomas Smelton, if this were he, was a small man dressed nattily in a linen suit the color of his sparse, white hair, a pale pink shirt and a blood red ascot. Over this he had slipped some sort of ancient battle dress consisting of chain mail sewed haphazardly to strips of leather with a miniskirt of animal fur. At his waist hung a small leather satchel and a sheathed dagger.

"Allow me to introduce myself. My name is Winston Wyc. I'm an historian."

"Yes, well . . . oh yes . . . my goodness, not *the* historian. The man sent to save the castle." The man clapped his hands together. "I'm delighted to meet you. Quite delighted."

"Then you know about me?"

"Of course. It was my idea to send for you in the first place."

"Oh."

"How did you find your way in here? It's a secret you know."

"From our meeting on the belvedere. When you left I realized you hadn't actually gone down the stairs. At first I was baffled, but by calculating the width of the steps and the tower, I realized that there was ample room for another set of stairs. You hadn't disappeared, you had merely taken another exit. It was up to me to find it."

"Very clever." Smelton gave a preemptory clap. "I knew you were the right man for the job."

"And you, sir, are . . . Thomas Smelton?"

"Yes indeed. Old Peeping Tom Smelton at your service. You will excuse my clumsiness. I've not been a host in years. One gets rusty. I'm sure there must be something I'm supposed to do." Drawing his face into a question mark, Smelton thought back on his Emily Post. Finally, he opened his eyes, composed himself and smiled. "Care for some tea?"

"Sure. Thanks."

Smelton motioned for Winston to sit and stepping behind a screen began banging pots. Sitting, Winston noticed the room for the first time. It was large and comfortably set out with overstuffed furniture, several oak library tables and in the corner an Empire sleigh bed. One wall was lined with bookshelves, another with cardboard boxes, the contents spilling out into the room. Next to the screen was another door.

"I heard a bit of a commotion earlier . . ." Smelton spoke from behind the screen. "Has there been another murder?"

"You know about that?"

"There's little goes on about the castle I don't know, Mr. Wyc." Smelton had reappeared with a china tea service which he placed on a pie crust table next to Winston. "Milk or sugar?"

"Just milk." Winston watched Smelton carefully pour milk into his tea. The man seemed to move at half speed as if his movements were discussed internally before being enacted externally. "Are there other secret entrances to your room?"

"Secret? You mean along the order of sliding panels and hidden doors? Not really. Actually my grandfather had that belvedere thing installed when he became enchanted with Norse mythology. I'm not sure how but it was used in an initiation rite of some sort for his Aesir Society. But by keeping a few portals under lock and key I'm pretty much in my own world. Privacy is everything to me."

"Does Conran know about the 'belvedere thing'?"

"Only you, dear boy."

Seemingly unaware of what he was doing, Smelton had remained next to Winston's chair, a dreamy smile on his lips, the teapot in one hand, a tea cozy in the other. Now he moved snail-like across the room to a table piled with small boxes. Setting down the pot and covering it with the cozy, Smelton took a moment to lift the lids of the boxes until he found the one he was seeking.

"I thought there might be a secret entrance over the

library. I was looking for one when I bumped into a man dressed as a nun."

"Did you? I'm sorry to disappoint you, but you've found the only one." Turning, Smelton took a second to regard Winston's outfit.

"Damn, I forgot. Diversionary dressing. Mind if I derobe?" Winston asked his host politely.

"Not at all. Just keep it clean." Smelton chuckled.

"I like *your* outer wear," said Winston.

"Ohhh . . . yes, well . . . I was involved in a little, how did you put it, diversionary dressing, myself. I had reached the chapter on granddad's Aesir Society and thought that by wearing his costume it might help. Rather primal don't you think?"

Winston smiled. "You're reading a book on the family?"

"Not reading . . . writing." Smelton had moved back across the room and with a calculated flourish presented the small, enamel box to Winston. "We have so much to discuss, Mr. Wyc and I fear so little time."

"You mean about historical designation?"

"Well . . . indirectly." Closing his eyes, Smelton took a moment to touch his temple with both hands. "If you open the box you will find a collection of remarkable little pills. The blue ones are valium and the brown ones. . . . Well, I don't actually remember. I call them droolers. Take one or two. They'll assist in relaxing you."

Winston stared into the box. There were many colors represented. "If you don't mind, I'll take a pass. I don't react well in an altered condition."

"Oh. You don't mind then if I do."

Shaking his head, Winston watched as Smelton selected a pill and, carefully placing it in his mouth, raised Winston's tea to his lips to wash it down.

"Yummy," said Smelton.

Great, thought Winston, here I am having leapt from the fire into the frying pan. If Thomas Smelton knew anything about the recent murders, then Winston had better ask him now for who knows where this gentleman's mind would be in another thirty minutes.

"Can I ask you a question, Mr. Smelton?"

"Certainly, Mr. Wyc, but first I have something to show you. Something I think you'll be very interested in seeing."

With that, Smelton turned and headed for the door next to the screen, his arms pumping slowly, his fur skirt swaying and his mind already in the other room.

Chapter 22

"Dr. Wallace sure looked pleased with herself tonight." Roberta peered around the diner as though the doctor might be taking notes in the next booth. "Seems anytime she can get one of the girls to break down she's happy."

"Part of the process," answered Mary.

"So she says. Poor Jenny."

"Jenny will be okay. It can be scary to suddenly realize that your family may have been dysfunctional."

"All that money and what good is it? Knowing when to stick out the right pinky's gotta be some mental burden. Hey!"

Roberta used her voice like a logger's maul except, in her case, she split eardrums. The waitress pretended she was deaf.

"When do we get to see your breakdown? That should be quite a show." Mary grinned to let Roberta know she wasn't altogether serious.

"My ass. Where's the damn waitress?" The waitress had ducked into the kitchen as Roberta swiveled in the booth. Roberta Cocca had the type of features that would have been burdensome for most women's faces, but on Roberta they combined to produce a very attractive lady. She would have been extremely pretty if she hadn't worn a sullen expression all the time. It was beginning to affect the lines of her face. "Denial's never been my problem. I can look back into my childhood and remember every crummy moment. *I* know who caused my unhappiness, and *I* know I'm obsessed by it. But what the fuck good does it do me?"

"It helps to know."

"I guess. And all this shit about 'boundary problems.' Wallace says I don't know where I end and my mother begins. Christ, my mother and I were welded early. I mean really, here we were the only women in a house with six men. Six major assholes. Talk about having a problem with individual ID in the context of family relations. Give me a break."

Mary wished Roberta would bring it down a few octaves. She was tired and Jenny's dramatics at the group tonight had really shaken her. Always uncomfortable when one of the other women in her group fell apart, Mary supposed hers was a normal reaction but it distressed her nonetheless. It was certainly better than Roberta's reaction. Why did the road to spiritual health have to be so embarrassing? And she certainly wasn't comfortable with Dr. Wallace's ideas on left-brain rationality. Mary had always considered herself a victim of circumstances and not defeat. Roberta's voice was only adding to the evening's tension.

"What do you want? I'll go find the waitress," offered Mary.

"Coffee. Just coffee. And some plain toast. No, make it buttered toast. That's it."

Placating the waitress, Mary made the order and slowly returned to the booth. Not only was Roberta and the group bothering her, she was worried about Winston. On the boat ride back to her cottage she realized how dangerous it was for him to be up at the castle. Although she was sure Winston had his act together, he certainly wasn't a match for the crazies roaming that nuthouse. The night wouldn't be over until she knew he was safe.

"Stuff's coming. Look . . . what about the guy pulled from the river? Got anything on him?" Mary lowered her voice hoping it would have its effect. Roberta's face clouded.

"Kevin Sanders." Roberta managed to come down to a normal level of speaking.

"That was his name?" Excitedly, Mary took out her notebook.

"Well . . . they're not sure." Roberta took a moment to arrange her thoughts. "Whoever deep-sixed the bastard didn't search him all that well. The guy was wearing two shirts and in the pocket of the one next to his body the boys found a few items of ID. A social security card, a driver's license and two credit cards. They were wrapped in one of those zip lock things you use for sandwiches so they hadn't been messed up in the water. Hey, that'd make for a great commercial. What do you think? The plastics people could use it on T.V. Police pull some body from a river and one of the boys finds this sandwich in the guy's coat, something like that, and it's still edible. Perfect seal. One of the cops could even take a bite."

Mary could only stare.

"Okay, forget it." Roberta shrugged.

"What about this guy?"

"The guy . . . well the picture on the driver's license was definitely him and the name used was Kevin Sanders."

"Who's . . ."

"Let me finish. The computer lady ran a tracer on the name and came up with two Kevin Sanders with police records. One's doing time at the moment out in Washington State and no one knows where the other one is. So here's our guy, right. Forget it. The prints don't match up. We're back to square one."

The waitress brought their order. Roberta managed to remain silent until the young woman left.

"How do they do that? I mean half your coffee is always in the saucer and looks like it's been there for a coupla days." Roberta gave the waitress's back an exaggerated sneer.

"Maybe we should ask her to join the group?" offered Mary.

"Yeah, right. Could take her apart then, hey?" Roberta smiled at the thought.

"So maybe this is some normal Kevin Sanders that's never been in trouble with the law."

"That might be true except that the social security number belongs to the con who's missing as does the credit card numbers."

"You mean the guy from the river has taken over the other guy's identity?"

Holding her shoulders in a shrug, Roberta turned her palms up in an expression of who knows.

"People sell their IDs, don't they?" asked Mary.

"They do and also identifications get stolen. Whatever happened here, this guy is definitely not Kevin Sanders the con."

"Could that ID have been put there to confuse somebody?"

"I don't know. The guy's prints have gone out over the line and also the Bureau. Plus I think the immigration boys. If the guy ever lived somewhere and worked, anywhere in the world, then we'll get a positive on him. Could take time though. And another thing."

"What's that?"

"The initial coroner's sheet said that the guy's bod had no obvious signs of misconduct."

"Tied to an anchor isn't too obvious?"

"It means that Sanders was clean. No extra holes or bruises or anything."

"He might have been poisoned?"

"He might have drowned."

"You mean . . . ?" Mary couldn't finish the thought.

"Yeah, I mean just that. It'll take ten days to get a full pathologist's report."

Thinking their own thoughts, the two women finished their coffee in silence. Mary's mind kept wandering back to the subject of Dutch Dace. It was time to have that heart-to-heart. If pursuing the story was going to get Dutch in trouble, then maybe it wouldn't get printed, but that would depend on his involvement. Did this fellow Sanders's death have any connection with the murder of Justin Barefoot?

"Okay, it's time for one hand to wash the other."

"What do you mean?" Mary knew exactly what Roberta meant. There was a price for everything.

"What? You think this info comes with just a smile and a cup of coffee?"

"The newspaper story?"

"Bingo, Mary dear." Roberta pulled some papers from her bag. "I've been putting down on paper all the stuff I've been hearing at the station plus the stuff that's S.O.P. concerning domestic quarrels, wife beatings, even rape."

"S.O.P.?"

"Standard Operating Procedures. There's rules

and then there's rules that only the boys know among themselves. You don't think cops treat women as second class citizens, then wait 'til you've read this."

Mary read the top sheet. "This verbatim?"

"Close as I could get. What do you want? I should carry a recorder into the station? They'd fry my ass."

"They're going to fry your ass anyway, Rob. You've got other people to verify this?"

"I tried to talk to the other women but they looked at me like I was nuts or something. Talk about feminism as a disease."

"Okay, I'll look over this and let you know."

"Soon, okay?"

"Soon. But be aware, this isn't going to happen anytime in the near future. We have to make sure of all our facts and we need corroboration. You don't come out with bad press on the police unless all the ducks are in a row. Sweetman knows this goes on?"

"What do you think? A department runs from the head down. The captain sets the tone and the attitude."

Mary had a hard time believing that, but Roberta was a friend. Besides, Mary knew from her own experience with the police that some of the boys still lived in the Paleolithic. That women were treated differently than men wasn't news.

"Look Rob, I've got to take off. I'm meeting someone at ten-thirty."

"A man-someone?"

"A story. Could be a really big scoop."

"No bowling alley tonight?"

Occasionally, Mary and Roberta would take their problems over to the Ho Bowl for a few drinks and a game. The physicalness of the bowling and the liquor helped them both relax. Lady's night out. Men and pin bashing.

"Afraid not. Thanks for the info. I'll read it tomorrow. Suddenly I have more stories than I can deal with properly."

"You're complaining?"

"Not me. Take care, Rob."

"Keep it in your pants, pal."

Outside, Mary stopped at the pay phone to call her cottage. Ten-thirty was here and she didn't want Winston thinking she was going to be late. The boy might try to take a swim on his own and that could be dangerous for him and the river. All she got was herself asking whoever called to leave a message. She talked into the phone after the beep in case he was reluctant to answer but he had either taken a walk or wasn't there. Maybe she could beat him home.

Chapter 23

Dutch eased up on the throttle, letting the *Hyorky* slow to a stop against the outgoing river. He had run far enough for his anger to dissipate. His sudden leaving; the engines full throttle up a busy river; it had all been childish but necessary. Dutch had wanted and needed the howl of the motors, the strong wind in his face and the quick distance—the isolation. Mary knew something or thought she did. It was unlike her to be in his place without telling him beforehand. It could only mean she was snooping. And worse, she had that Wyc fellow with her. Damn her, thought Dutch, feeling the anger rising again in his blood. Mary was not to know. She was his one link to the world as it should be lived, his redeeming factor. As long as Mary remained innocent, he remained innocent. As long as she thought him incapable of wrongdoing, he could live a lie and feel no guilt. And of course, wrongdoing was in the seeing, hearing and speaking of the beholder. But that was about to change. Dutch knew he could get her to stop, could use their friendship to warn her away, but then she would have to know everything and that would mean dragging her into the lie and putting her in jeopardy. It would mean the end of pretending.

Leaving the pilothouse to drop anchor, Dutch remembered Mary as a child. He almost smiled. Mary had cut her hair really short once before, when she was ten years old. She had read in a book somewhere that only men and boys were allowed to go to sea, that women on board were bad luck. So Mary had whacked her hair off and took to wearing boy's clothes. Mary's mother had had to get Dutch to explain that that was the old days and didn't hold true for the present, although Dutch knew that wasn't true. Even today many of the guys had problems with women on board their ships. A distraction, they'd say. Dutch had always enjoyed having the ladies aboard. He could talk to them about subjects other than sports or fishing . . . or other women, topics his fellow fishermen could talk about endlessly. Everyone said Dutch was a loner. Well, where they were concerned, it was true. Most of the time he was bored silly with the company. Shipping out might never have continued for Verplanck Dace except that early in his maritime career, he found a loyal companion. The sea had become his friend, his confidante, its energy and boundlessness comforting and real. The ocean could be unpredictable but never thoughtless, maybe frightening at times but never oppressive. It could take a man to his physical and mental limits and even beyond but it wasn't testing or discerning. The ocean was what it was, and if a man could live with his fear and keep his sea legs, then he would weather the storm and find himself better for it.

The ocean could also soothe and heal. The salt air, the comforting rhythm, the vast quiet, all combined to ease a man's soul and restore him. Dutch had

216

always enjoyed coming home, experiencing the Hudson, visiting with his new friends. But within months the urge would creep back into his nights and before long he'd once again be sitting on a bench in the union hall off Battery Park in New York waiting, not for a ship really, but for the ocean.

Watching the anchor slip beneath the water, Dutch eyed the other and wondered about Mary. How she could have connected the one wrapped around Sanders with the one he had bought, he wasn't sure, but it was not a good sign. If she was asking questions about the damn thing then the police might be next. Another anchor needed to be found and quickly. Dutch would have to liberate an anchor up in Albany later that night after the drop-off. He hadn't made it this far by being careless about even the slightest thing.

Studying the water, Dutch thought back over the last two years. In the beginning it had all seemed so straightforward and, like the Hudson River of his childhood, so clear. Now, everything, including the river, was murky and dirty. Mom had said to give it a few years and if the pressure became too much then he could quit. Well, maybe the time had come. The possibility of going to jail had always been in the back of his mind but the actuality of it had seemed remote. Now there were too many people involved and some of them were dying, and suddenly time in the stir *was* a possibility. To spend the end of his life in a small cell far from any living waters would be his death. The keepers of the deep currents who waited to take him off around the world would never hold him and he would wind up in an even worse cell, the landlocked confines of a pine box, far from the watery heaven that he had always envisioned as his eternity.

Dutch moved back to the pilothouse. Mom would get one more trip out of him. He wouldn't desert her now but he would make it clear that he was retiring after tonight's boat ride. Would take the money and disappear. Mom would understand. They had known each other a long time, and if "friend" was too strong a word to use in describing their relationship, then "respect" would do.

Being out on the river made Dutch feel better and cleared his mind for the decision making. A long talk with Mary would be next. That would take care of the rest of his burden and then he'd check out. The money had been good and Dutch knew of an island where he could buy in. With his merchant marine pension he could spend those last years happy, talking to the end of his fishing line and not to the shadows thrown by vertical bars.

Pulling out his bottle of Jack Daniel's, Dutch watched the sun sink behind the high bluff on his right and hoped his "cargo" was ready. He hoped that tonight would run smoothly and as ordinary as the outgoing tide. Until then he would rest out here on the river and bide his time. He'd have a drink and enjoy the changing colors on the rock face of the far bank, let the slap of water against the *Hyorky* lull him back to another time.

Chapter 24

Winston put the typed pages back on the table. "I'm impressed, Mr. Smelton."

"I knew you'd appreciate what I've done. It's taken a long time but everything is almost in order. You wouldn't believe the number of boxes gone through. The trunks, the closets, the pockets of old clothes even. The phone calls, the letters, the interviews. Endless. One of the Smeltons, my grandfather's brother George, began once to write a history of the Smelton family but didn't get very far. Seems there wasn't much to write about." Smelton chuckled. "He didn't understand what he had. But he did interview all the family at that point and collect certain memorabilia. That was a great help."

Winston nodded. "Did your family ever throw anything away?"

"Obviously very lazy in that exercise. As were the servants. Never any good help in this part of the woods. Turned out to be a blessing of sorts."

After tea, Smelton had taken Winston into another larger room that held what he proudly referred to as: *The History.* A massive collection of paper and photographs centered around the world of Smelton Castle. Winston had been shown a letter that had been sent in nineteen hundred inquiring about the land on the Hudson and its availability; a diary informing of the search in Scotland for a suitable castle and its eventual purchase; correspondence concerning the dismantling and shipping of the castle and the problems ensued in shipping and reconstruction; histories of servants and local families from nineteen hundred and two to the late fifties. Photographs were shown of the castle being rebuilt and its changes over the years; of everyone who ever lived or worked in the castle; of the Hudson River and New Holland and anything of significance in the immediate area. Thomas Smelton had collected a historian's dream: the entire history, physical and human, of a household from its beginning to its end. And not only the important moments but also the minutiae of running the castle, like how many eggs were bought for the week of June fifth, nineteen hundred and twelve; or the cost of forty cords of wood in nineteen hundred and twenty to heat the estate; or an account of the difficult birth of a servant's daughter. Here it all was: organized, systematized, orchestrated into neatly arranged drawers and boxes, waiting for . . . what? Smelton had shown Winston his book which was oddly enough completely disorganized and unreadable. A jumble of words and history. Smelton had asked Winston if he'd like to assist in writing the history for, as Winston realized, the man had figured out that he couldn't do it alone. It was all too much for Winston to think about at the present.

"You say you're working on a chapter about the Aesir Society?"

"Yes, the Aesir Society. Phillip Smelton, my grandfather, was into Snorri Sturluson's . . . I love that name . . . the *Prose Edda.* Do you know it? The *Gylfaki* . . . the *Gylfanin* . . . I can never pronounce it properly but it changed his life. He founded this group and they used to meet here at the castle. Old Phillip rearranged much of the castle because of his interest in Scandinavia."

"I've seen the dining room. Very interesting."

"Oh yes. The boys would meet for two weeks once a year and, dressed like I am now, wage battle. The gods of the Aesir would fight the gods of ebil . . . evil. Excuse me."

"I think that battle is still being waged. You don't happen to know anything about these recent deaths, do you?" The hell with subtlety, thought Winston.

Smelton grinned his dreamy grin and looked knowingly into the middle distance. "Can't say that I do, Mr. Wyc."

Winston didn't believe him. But then, if Conran was his buddy and protector, why would he implicate the man? Heavy footsteps could be heard on the stairs above them.

"Sounds like someone running on the stairs," said Smelton looking up. "No one ever runs here."

"Looking for me, probably," offered Winston. "You say I'm the only one who knows about the secret entrance?"

"Only you."

Shouts could be heard. Smelton rubbed his hands together and chuckled, an old wizard about to wreak havoc.

"Let's take to the tunnels and see what's going on."

"Tunnels?"

"Passageways really. They weren't built to be secret, but you wall up an entrance here, block an exit there, and voilà! There you have a secret passageway. I did that before I sold the place. Clever, hey?" Another knavish chuckle.

"Nothing like planning ahead. You feel like traveling about?" Winston wasn't all that comfortable with Smelton's glazed features.

"Certainly, Mr. Wyc." As he motioned for Winston to fall in behind, Smelton's face lit up with a brilliant idea. "Oh . . . perhaps I should bring a flask of something stalwart. Some shooting sherry . . . or better yet, the twenty-five year old Glenfiddich. Who knows how long we may be out?"

Winston's look was discouraging.

"Hmmm, right. Well, tally ho." Smelton took off with Winston close at his heels.

"You say it was your idea to get me here?"

"Yes, I did some asking around. I've become acquainted with several historians over the years because of my book. They recommended you."

"No kidding." Winston felt honored and more than a little surprised. He knew he was one of the few architectural historians working outside of the academic community but he hadn't known that they appreciated his endeavors on the part of civilian interest groups. Winston wondered who had recommended him. "That's nice to hear."

"I was told that if anyone could swave . . ." Smelton stopped and smacked his lips together. ". . . could *save* the castle, it would be you. Now I understand that might not be the case." Smelton's face became grim and thoughtful.

"Well . . . actually, now that I've seen *The History* I'll have to rethink my position. I think it makes for a stronger argument than trying to designate the castle and the grounds alone. It's a remarkable collection of history, dealing with the castle's relationship to the surrounding community for almost a century. I would think the local academic and historical groups would love to have it. We could use it as a bribe of sorts.''

"Oh that's wonderful. I *knew* you could do it."

The two men passed through a low door and into a room taken up almost entirely with a set of stone steps.

"These match the stairs outside the library," exclaimed Winston.

"Correct. We're on the other side of the dining hall. I hated to hide these but there was nothing I could do." Defensively, Smelton cocked his head. "No one seems to miss them."

Amazing thought Winston. The place is so big, so convoluted that a quarter of the castle could be walled off and nobody seemed to notice. He followed Smelton up the stairs.

"I don't mean to dampen the good news, but I'm not sure I'm welcome about the castle anymore. This nun I mentioned earlier, the one masquerading as a man, has a gun and I got the definite feeling he wished to use it on me. I think I'm going to have to abandon Smelton Castle for now."

"Dear me. I'd forgotten about that." Smelton stopped to consider what Winston had said.

"There's something else going on at the castle, Mr. Smelton. Something that has nothing to do with pampering wealthy ids. Conran and the staff are not very happy about my bumping into this nun."

"Yes, nuns . . . look, I could talk to Michael. He listens to me."

I bet, thought Winston. "I think it's bigger than both of us. You don't happen to know what that activity might be, do you?"

Smelton fumbled with the satchel at his waist. "They do seem to have a big turnover in nuns but I never gave it much thought."

"I'm trying to help you, Mr. Smelton. If what Conran is doing is illegal, you might lose the castle. If you came forward now, the authorities would be very appreciative."

"Lose the castle? Conran promised me the authorities wouldn't find out."

"Find out what?"

Narrowing his eyes, Smelton stared into the dark, his fingers clasping and unclasping the dagger's hilt. Winston realized that if he was going to make it out of the castle alive he'd better stay on the good side of old Tom. Suggesting that the man might lose his beloved castle was not helping his cause. Reason had no place in this conversation.

"*Squeaking* of *tribes* . . ." Smelton looked bemused and cleared his throat. "Sorry. Speaking of bribes, I don't suppose you'd be above such . . . eh . . . behavior, would you, Mr. Wyc?"

"What do you mean?"

"If you don't mind my saying, you strike me as an historian first and a citizen of the community second. Is this a false assumption?"

"Depends." Winston thought he knew where Smelton was going with this idea and he didn't like it.

"I have oodles of money and where my castle, my *History* is concerned . . ." Smelton's voice trailed off.

Smelton had a new look in his eyes. Behind the

obvious drug glaze there lurked something else, something menacing. Winston checked his watch for an excuse. "Goodness, it's getting late. Would you mind terribly if we discussed this in the morning? This is all too much for me, too much information at one time, you understand. I promise I won't mention what I've said to anyone until we've all had a little chat."

Smelton didn't understand too much at the moment, Winston had a feeling.

"You promise?"

Winston nodded. He'd promise the life of his dear old granny at this point. Smelton gave Winston's nod a long consideration.

"Good. Then let's continue to sneak around. Follow me."

Winston waited for Smelton to move. After a full minute he began to wonder if his leaving might not be better accomplished on his own. Starting to move back down the stairs, Winston was stopped by Smelton's small voice.

"Not that way."

Winston fell in line once again. "You going to be okay?"

"I'm okay, Mr. Wyc, not to worry. I'm feeling quite chipper now. Quite chipper indeed." As if to underscore the point Smelton shook his hips back and forth and clapped twice.

At the top of the stairs, Smelton took a left and led Winston into a passageway that mimicked the darkened hall on the other side of the dining area. This hall also had the peepholes. The two men peeped. Leaning into one another at a table sat Conran and Cynthia Shea whispering and looking about at the walls.

"Can you hear what they're saying?" asked Winston.

Smelton shook his head no. The nun-with-the-gun came clamoring into the hall.

"No sign of the bastard," he yelled from twenty feet away. Winston realized the man had a decidedly British Isles accent.

"Keep it down, man. The walls have ears . . . and eyes." Conran rose and addressed the wall opposite Winston. "You up there, Thomas? Damnit where in the hell are you? We need you at the moment. The castle is in danger."

Whispering, Smelton grabbed Winston's arm. "What does he mean?"

"Because of me."

"You? Oh, yeah . . . ?" The menacing look came back into Smelton's gaze.

"You promised to get me out of here," Winston said quickly.

"I did?"

Smelton was looking more and more confused. Conran's voice could be heard shouting up at the ceiling. How much longer Smelton would stay in one piece, Winston didn't know, but he had to get out of there now before the man convinced himself or was convinced by others that Winston should remain. Without coaxing, Smelton moved away and down the hall. Silently, Winston followed.

Two doors and many stairs later, Winston found himself being escorted through a damp, narrow passageway that curved slightly upward. High above them light filtered in from an opening. It was the second such opening they had passed under. The movement had seemed to bring a bounce back into Smelton's gait.

226

"Are those for ventilation?" Winston pointed up at the light. Smelton chuckled.

"Heavens no. Those were originally garderobes."

"What's that?"

"Medieval toilets. Waste fell down to this chute we're now in and was flushed away with water. But not to worry, it was never used for that purpose here."

"Where are we headed by the way?"

"This leads to a system of passages that will take us eventually out the north end of the castle, in the rear. Shall we continue?"

Abruptly the chute ended. A set of metal rungs set into the stone led up to three rough boards which, when moved aside, gave access to a narrow room where at one end stood a metal wheel wrapped by chain linkage that disappeared up into the ceiling.

"What's that?" asked Winston.

"*Yesh . . . wes.* Excuse me a minute." Smelton leaned his head against the stone wall for a full two minutes. Winston had begun to worry when suddenly Smelton came back to life. "Sorry about that. An epiphany. What is it you wanted to know?"

"Where are we?"

"Oh yes, well . . . originally this small space would have provided two functions. At one time the passage we were just in would have been interrupted by a strong, wooden door that could be manipulated from this space. When raised it would have allowed water from a moat or some water supply to flush out the chute. Early plumbing. The wheel there when it turns opens and closes the portcullis that blocks the main entrance. Conran, bless him, had the thing electrified." Smelton moved across to the wheel.

"Right behind here is a ladder that will take us up to a passageway that runs all around the castle in the curtain walls. It's from there that you can get to the battlements and what is called the wall walk."

Above the wheel room was a larger room which housed the portcullis. The gate was in the closed position. Scattered about the room's floor were four inch holes that looked down on the entrance underpass.

"What are these holes? For spying?" Winston knelt down to peer through one.

"Meurtrières. There're other rooms that have them. The solar has a few, and the old armory."

"Meurtrières? I'm afraid my French is a little rusty."

"Murder holes. You could shoot the enemy in the head as he entered the castle. The old boys were masters at killing."

Winston thought the new boys were pretty good at it themselves. The tower housing the portcullis was transected by a passage that ran within the curtain wall of the castle. Every fifteen feet was a narrow lancet window on either side that offered good cross ventilation. Winston stopped to take in a good inhale of fresh air.

"I feel very Jacobean in these surroundings." Striking a pose, Winston began reciting:

> "Men must endure
> Their going hence, even as their coming
>   hither:
> Ripeness is all."

"Very good, Mr. Wyc. *King Lear* I believe."
"That's right." Winston was impressed with Mr.

Smelton's knowledge of Shakespeare. "I must con-
fess it's really the only play of the Bard's I've ever
read. A college course."

"Yes . . . let me see." Smelton screwed his face into
a maze of concentration.

"I am a very foolish fond old man,
Fourscore and upward, not an hour more or less;
And, to deal plainly,
I fear I am not in my perfect mind."

Truer words were never spoken thought Winston
who silently applauded Smelton's modest bow.

"Thank you. I adore Shakespeare. I guess being
brought up in a castle one would have to. Shall we
continue? Now this passage was not part of the
original castle." Smelton started back down the
passage. "Originally the castle was built with two
masonry walls fifteen feet apart that were filled with
rubble. Great granddad decided to leave the rubble
back in Scotland and construct this passageway
instead."

"Good thinking," said Winston to himself. Peering cautiously out one of the lancet windows,
Winston could see two nuns hurrying across the
parking area toward the main gate. He stepped back
as they looked up in his direction. Damn. His
recitation was probably heard down in the courtyard.
Smelton's voice came down from the darkened passageway encouraging Winston to keep up for they
were almost there. Almost where? wondered Winston
who was beginning to doubt his decisions of the last
hour. If Smelton and Conran were such good
buddies, why were they scurrying around the castle
in Hallowe'en costumes avoiding contact with any-

one? And who was the enemy? Could these be the people who killed Justin Barefoot or the man found in the Hudson River?

"Mr. Wyc. Come along, please. While the halls are empty."

There was one way to find answers to all these questions. Winston had only to continue trusting his life to a crazed little man dressed like "Hagar the Horrible" high on god knows what. Seemed simple enough. Heaving a deep sigh, Winston hurried toward Peeping Tom Smelton and whatever confrontation awaited. Ahhh, the life of the architectural historian, he thought. Never a dull minute.

"This door leads out into a hallway. Directly opposite is another door that leads to a flight of stairs that will take you down to a tunnel that runs under the castle and out the back."

"I think I've been in that tunnel."

"Good, then you know where it leads. I'll make sure the coast is clear."

Stepping through the door, Smelton did a farcical nod up and down the hallway. He grabbed Winston's arm as he went by. "Mr. Wyc. You see a crazed old man and maybe that's the case, but like Lear's, my craziness has its underpinning of reason. I would do anything to keep my castle, *my History* . . . and I have. Remember your promise. Go ahead."

The door at the end of the hall slammed open revealing Conran and the nun.

"I knew it. I knew it. Hold it right there you ingrate, you mouse turd, you sniveling wrecker of all that is peaceful."

Winston turned back to Smelton but the old man was gone. Moving quickly across the hall, Winston was through the door. Hesitating for a second,

Winston looked for a way to lock the door. Nothing. He bounded down the stairs. Shouts could be heard behind him. Could those invectives have been hurled at him? Reaching the tunnel, Winston made for the back stairs and freedom.

"Not so fast, Winston."

Winston leapt at the sudden voice coming from the darkness beside him. Out from the shadows stepped Eric Shrove wearing his "Doughboy of the Damned" face and holding a small but deadly looking revolver.

"You went and found Mr. Smelton without me. Not very nice, Winston. Not nice at all."

Boots pounded on the stairs. "Don't take it so personally, Eric. You were in a meeting. Look pal, I got to get the hell out of here."

"Yes, the meeting. Well, I'm here now."

"I can see that. What's with the gun?"

The outside door to the tunnel banged shut. Footsteps could be heard coming toward them.

"Quick. With me, Winston." Eric wiggled his revolver for emphasis. The two men made the bend in the tunnel just as the door from the hallway flew open. Eric motioned Winston through an open door. Winston recognized it as the one he had used earlier that led back to the reception area. Eric slid a bolt tight behind them as Winston started up the stairs.

"That will keep them busy for a moment. Keep moving, please." Another gun wiggle.

"I'm going to build myself a house someday, thought Winston, and there won't be one damn door in the whole place. Or a hallway for that matter. And what was with his friend Eric? Seemed everyone here had a gun except Winston. Was the gun for protection or was it meant . . . ? "Doughboy of the Damned" sure wanted to get his hands on Thomas

231

Smelton. Suddenly Winston knew. It was so obvious. He turned back to Eric.

"Could you answer a question for me, Eric?"

"Sure. Depends."

"Where does one put the cash flow chart? With the debit or credit sheets?"

Eric smiled. "Fuck you." Pushing ahead of Winston, Eric peeped through the door to the reception room. With a curt nod of his head, he indicated that Winston should go first. Halfway across the room, they were suddenly in a crowd. A large man in a lumberman's jacket stepped from the shadows of the entrance hall. Miss Pinklingill and the Engine came out of the conference room. And Sister Kerry threw open the door to the office.

"Going somewhere, Eric?" asked Miss Pinklingill in her small but authoritative voice. "I can see the meeting really upset you. A shame. I was so hoping we could work together."

"How gracious, Melody, but as you can also see, I'm the one with the gun. Now if you'd like to step aside, the historian and I would like to leave. We feel we've overstayed our welcome."

"This is nonsense. Who are you going to shoot? An old lady, an unarmed nun? What bravery. Mr. Shrove here wanted to shoot our dear old Thomas, did you know that, Mr. Wyc?"

"It had recently occurred to me, yes."

"I'm sorry that you've had to become mixed-up in all this foolishness, Mr. Wyc." Miss Pinklingill had taken out her pocket watch. "Oh my, it's getting late. The *Hyorky* must be somewhere by morning and you're delaying things, Mr. Shrove. Now be sensible and put that thing down. You're not going anywhere."

"Like hell . . ." Eric moved cautiously toward the doorway. "Move, Rolly, or I'll shoot." The big man looked terrified by the whole situation. He inched out of the way.

"You move, Rolly, and you're fired." Miss Pinklingill hit her arm rest a solid little blow.

"What?" Rolly looked from one face to another, pleading for sanity to make an entrance. It did, somewhat, with the shouts of Conran from the mezzanine above them. Clamoring down the stone steps, he was followed by the fake nun and two real nuns Winston had never seen. For a second, Winston thought Eric might begin shooting, but the man came to his senses and put his gun hand down.

"Take his gun," said Miss Pinklingill to Rolly.

"Well, well . . . the comedy team of Wyc and Shrove. Quite the little chase, yes indeed." Conran huffed himself in between the two men. After a few deep inhales he continued. "How extraordinary we should all arrive here at the same time. Fate has her little ways."

"Where's Cynthia?" asked Miss Pinklingill.

"She's down at the boat," answered Conran. "Where we'll all be in a moment. Goodness. All this tramping about has unraveled me. Much too much activity."

"Not for nothing, folks . . ." Winston wondered where he fit into all this. ". . . but I'm having a hard time putting all of this together."

"Understandable, Winston. There's much going on, too much. I must prepare my friend here for a long trip . . ." Conran indicated the nun-with-the-gun. ". . . I would appreciate your sitting with Melody for a short while as I get things ready. Perhaps she can provide a few answers. Mr. Shrove,

233

you will come with me. We must talk in private."

With that, Conran and the nun hustled Eric out the door. Rolly motioned for Winston to sit.

"I'm not sure I can answer your questions, Mr. Wyc. But I'll certainly listen."

"Miss Pinklingill, I wonder . . ."

"Mom, Mr. Wyc. Call me Mom. Everyone does."

Chapter 25

Mary put down the bottle of Jack Daniel's. A third drink was not what she needed. Winston hadn't stood her up; he was in trouble. She had two options: call the police or get her ass over to the retreat. As any good reporter not ready to turn in their press card would do, Mary pulled on jeans and a black sweatshirt and headed down to the water. No matter what might have occurred between her and Dutch, he was still her friend and as long as he was near, Mary felt safe about entering the retreat grounds.

A decision had been made and Mary felt the better for it. Banging around the house waiting for Winston had been driving her nuts; at least now she was taking action. All her reporting instincts were on edge, alive with the knowledge that a short distance away something newsworthy was happening. What that might be she wasn't sure but the fact that Winston was probably in the center of the trouble made her all the more anxious. Winston might not be the love of her life but she certainly did like the guy.

The twenty-five horsepower outboard sounded loud in the still night. Hopefully all but Dutch would be up at the castle. Mary could have driven to the retreat but the gate would be locked by now and by the time she had hidden her car and found a way down to the castle it was quicker to take the river route. Usually Mary liked being out on the water at night, particularly one as clear and starry as this night, but this evening the silent river looked not only dark but threatening. To the east of New Holland could be seen the glow of the rising moon which was two nights away from being full. Mary would have no trouble seeing her way to the castle but the brilliance of the night sky might work against her. She wouldn't worry about that now.

The *Hyorky* had returned. Mary felt the rumble of its powerful engines long before she actually spotted it moored by the boathouse. She wasn't sure why it would be idling at this time of night, but it probably wasn't a good sign. Someone or something was preparing to leave and midnight was not normal traveling time. Mary had gone over and over in her mind what Roberta had told her concerning the body of Kevin Sanders, if indeed that turned out to actually be the person found wrapped around the anchor. Roberta had said there was no obvious cause of death. What if the person hadn't been murdered but had died of natural causes? What if Dutch had simply buried a man at sea rather than have to bring him back to land and go through the complications of an earthly interment? If that was the case, then the question to be asked was not why he was murdered, but why did his body have to be hidden? As far as Dutch Dace was concerned, this made more sense to Mary. Dutch, she was sure, wouldn't kill anyone but he might go to extremes to hide the evidence of some particular wrongdoing. What Mary had to find out was the specifics of that wrongdoing. Something Roberta had said in passing kept sticking in Mary's mind. Just two words that didn't add up to anything specific but to Mary's reporter instincts, they held the key to the whole situation. Where Justin Barefoot fit into all this was the big mystery for Mary, but she was beginning to think that the two deaths had nothing to do with each other.

Choosing a spot a hundred yards down the shore, Mary tied her skiff to the bank and walked the remaining distance to the *Hyorky*. The side of the boathouse near the boat was in dark shadow and Mary could stand here unnoticed. A car she didn't recognize was parked by the dock and Dutch's profile could be seen in the main salon on the boat talking to someone Mary couldn't see. No one else seemed to be around. Crouching, Mary ran from the safety of the shadows to the side of the boat. No alarm was sounded. Unless someone came onto the dock from the direction of the castle, she was hidden. Cautiously making her way along the gunwale, Mary chose a spot just below the pilothouse ladder and quickly, quietly rolled her body over the side and down onto the deck of the boat. The rumble of the engines covered her entry onto the *Hyorky* but she had to be careful not to rock the boat to her side as she moved. Although she wasn't that heavy, it didn't take much weight to roll a boat. Slowly Mary inched up the ladder and splayed out on the roof of the forward cabin. Narrow ventilation slits provided her with a constricted view of the main salon. Directly in front of her was the back of Dutch's head and sitting on a banquette before him was Cynthia Shea. In this position below the pilothouse, Mary was out in the open and it made her nervous. If they were waiting for someone that person would probably be along very soon. Hopefully they would arrive by car for a vehicle's headlights would give her ample warning.

Placing her ear by the opening, Mary could hear snatches of conversation above the engine noise. Cynthia was talking.

". . . Mom won't be all that . . . understand, of course . . . the whole thing has . . ."

". . . worked out. Rolly can take over. He's familiar with the routine. I've got to . . . the end of shad season . . . I mean," answered Dutch.

". . . not the one . . ." Rising, Cynthia Shea went over to a window. "Where could they be?"

Dutch said something Mary couldn't hear and walked from the salon. Mary rolled over the cabin roof and down onto the deck away from the dock. Dutch's weight could be felt climbing the ladder to the pilothouse. There was a matching ladder on her side of the boat and, hesitating for only a second, Mary was into the pilothouse and sitting on the floor looking up into the startled face of Dutch Dace. His expression changed from confusion to apprehension and finally to incredulous amusement.

"You're worse than a hungry black fly," whispered Dutch who made a quick inspection of the surrounding night. "This is not a good time to be here."

"What's going on? Who's leaving?"

Dutch crouched down beside Mary. "You can have the whole thing but not now. It's dangerous, do you hear? Now get your ass over the side." The lights of an approaching car could be seen sweeping the roof of the pilothouse. "Great. Keep down and keep quiet." Dutch rose and took the ladder back down to the deck.

Mary immediately scurried across the floor and knelt. She used a slicker hanging by the starboard porthole to hide her face as she peeked at the scene outside. The castle mini-van had pulled up to the dock. Conran sat on the driver's side talking to a nun

238

in the front seat. Two people sat in the back. Cynthia Shea had joined Dutch on the dock. Stepping from the van, Conran motioned for Cynthia to join him a short distance away. The two bent their heads in quiet conversation. The nun stepped from the van and with a quick motion pulled off her wimple. It took Mary a moment to realize that the nun was a man and that he had taken a gun from the front seat. The side door of the mini-van slid open and out tumbled the missing Winston Wyc. Rolly stumbled out after Winston. The three stood quietly by the van looking nervous and waiting for Conran.

"Could we talk to you please?" Cynthia made a "come here" motion with her hand to Dutch who joined her and Conran off to the side. After a minute, Dutch hesitantly made his way over to the boathouse and, switching on a light, disappeared into the storage area beneath his apartment. As Conran came back over to the mini-van, Cynthia got into the car by the dock and with a spattering of gravel drove hurriedly up the drive. Dutch had reappeared with what looked like a spool of clothesline. He gave a quick glance up at the pilothouse before joining Conran. Mary couldn't hear what was being said but Winston was becoming more agitated. From his gestures, Mary realized that he took exception to the idea of being tied with the clothesline. The fellow dressed as a nun said something that convinced Winston to cooperate. Conran and Dutch were now heading toward the boat and Mary could hear Dutch's raised voice.

". . . in the pilothouse. But I see no need for you to come up. I'll bring the charts down to the salon."

"Why bother, Mr. Dace? I've always loved the feel of the pilothouse, the power of it as it were, the wide window with its commanding view, the instrumentation." Conran played with the syllables of this last word, hitting them hard and stretching them out.

"Whatever."

Sliding across the floor on her stomach, Mary waited until she felt the two men board and then quickly she eased herself over the threshold of the door and down onto the deck. Unless Conran looked directly out the door and down, he wouldn't see her. She could imagine what Dutch must be going through just before entering the pilothouse. He was the first to speak.

"I . . . eh . . ."

"Something wrong, Mr. Dace?"

"No, no. I thought I had left something here but I just remembered it's still up in the apartment. Here are the charts for the immediate area."

Mary could hear a rustling of fine paper.

"What part of the river would you suggest, Mr. Dace?"

Dutch hesitated before speaking. "Look, Mr. Conran, I really don't think I can do this. Killing people was never part of the deal."

"I know that, but things are . . . what's the word . . . extraordinary at the moment. There's an international network of people who rely on our being here, Mr. Dace. We can't let them down because of a few misfits. Think of the broader picture. Now where do you suggest?"

Dutch took a full minute to respond. "Along here would probably be okay."

"Probably? We can't have more bodies popping up. That was a real faux pas, Mr. Dace."

"That was not my fault. And I did not kill that man. He died all by himself. He was sick and you knew that."

"I'm not casting blame. No, no . . . I know this is

difficult and I want you to know that I . . . that we all, understand your wanting to jump ship, as it were. Do this one last thing and you can retire in quiet and grace." Conran's voice had become too smooth, too ingratiating. It was not the attitude to take with Dutch. Why he had gone along with it this far was a mystery to Mary unless he himself felt threatened. It was obvious that they meant to deep-six Winston. Leaning her back into the cool metal of the salon cabin wall, Mary wondered about international groups and what they might want with retreats and nuns. Smelton Castle must be a way station of some sort, a stop over for . . . Mary smiled. Roberta's words came back to her: immigration boys. Harboring. What an appropriate wrongdoing for a retreat on the Hudson River. Conran's voice brought her back to her senses. Mary had to make it into Dutch's apartment without being seen. A phone call right now could save everyone a lot of trouble. With a quick look around, Mary moved down the deck and away from the pilothouse. Removing her tennis shoes, she slithered over the side and dropped into the cool water of the Hudson. The last time she had felt this watery caress there had been a man alongside her and that man was now in danger. Pulling herself along the hull, Mary realized that Dutch might not see the rising sun himself. If he could stall setting out for just twenty minutes, then all might be saved. What a story. What a headline!

Chapter 26

"So you see, Mr. Wyc, there really *is* no other solution. There is too much at stake."

Spreading her hands over her lap, Melody Pinklingill offered Winston a good-natured smile in lieu of a reprieve. Winston was to be sacrificed for the larger good, that is, to prevent his exposing the retreat as part of a network that sheltered and moved terrorists on the run to safe havens in the United States. Miss Pinklingill had used the words "political refugees" but Winston had gotten the drift.

"I take it the promise of a gentleman means nothing around here?" As he spoke, Winston wondered if Rolly would actually shoot him if he walked out the door. The man looked more frightened than he did.

"There are no more gentlemen, Mr. Wyc. They went the way of the horse drawn carriage and the bustle. And I'd stop eyeing the door if I was you. It's not Rolly you have to worry about; it's Sister Mary. Isn't that true, dear?"

The Engine rolled her face into a grin. Winston wasn't quite sure what it was he had to worry about;

there seemed to be no weapon and he could certainly out pace the chubby little nun, but something about the woman's grin kept him in his seat. Whatever menace she possessed couldn't be pleasant, so Winston would bide his time. Between the castle and the river he was hopeful of finding an escape. If he could get alone with Rolly he might have a chance.

Conran and Liam, as the man-nun was called, reentered the reception room without Eric Shrove.

"Where's Eric?" asked Winston as if it mattered.

"Eric's not well and has taken to his room," said Conran. "And no, Winston, we haven't slit his plump little throat. *Yet.* Mr. Shrove has lots to tell us but I'm afraid he's being stupidly reticent. I think he's more terrified of his boss than he is of me."

"Should he be?"

"Mr. Shrove . . . incidentally, this person is not Mr. Shrove, Winston. This person, whoever he is, came here misrepresenting himself. Not nice at all. This person made a logistical error, for he thought none of us had ever met the real Eric Shrove. I'm surprised Justin Barefoot hadn't known that I myself had once met the real Mr. Shrove at a gathering in Washington. At first I was quite taken aback to see this Eric, for I remembered him as tall and rather advanced in age. But, I thought, I'd go along with the little game and see what came of it."

"Is that why you killed Mr. Barefoot?" Winston wished he could sound more upset, but the truth was he felt only tired and wilted.

"I didn't kill Justin, Winston. Fact is, we don't know who murdered the poor man. Certainly set off a sad series of events." Conran said this last part in a loud voice to the ceiling.

"We could probably make an educated guess, though," offered Melody Pinklingill, motioning for the Engine to move her from the room. "But we won't."

"Taking off?" asked Conran.

"I certainly am. And so should you. Liam has a date and he shouldn't be tardy. Good luck, son."

"Thank you, Mom." Still dressed in his habit, Liam gave what looked like a quick curtsy in Miss Pinklingill's direction.

"Okay, Winston, let's go fishing." Conran gave Winston a special bear hug.

"What's the bait? Me?"

"Lure, Winston. What's the lure? I've always liked that word better. Bait smacks of worm farms and fetid little shacks hugging some river bank. The Oblates of Tranquil Deliverance is a class act. We use only lures."

"Mr. Dace tie them for you?"

"Tie them? You've got me there, Winston. Now let's move along, please."

Idling outside in the parking area was a mini-van with the retreat's logo painted on the doors.

"Rolly, you sit in the back with Mr. Wyc. Liam will ride shotgun. You're the historian, Winston. What's that mean? Shotgun."

"It has to do with stage coaches, Mr. Conran."

"Stage coaches? Oh yes . . . of course. Well, how appropriate. Will a nine millimeter pistol do? In case we run into any . . . Indians?"

Winston only nodded.

"Sorry we never got to take that tour," added Conran. "There's lots of fascinating nooks and crannies scattered about the old castle, but then you probably saw a few of them first hand, as it were."

Winston was through talking. All his energy, whatever he could muster, would go into discovering and acting upon a means of escape. He had hoped the trip to the boathouse would be on foot and now he would have to wait until they had reached the river. A crazy man had shot him in the stomach the last time he had worked in the countryside and he had survived. Winston planned on surviving this time too.

Over his shoulder, Winston gave the inner bailey of the castle one more inspection. It really did take a different time, a different economy, for someone to take down a structure this large, transport it over an ocean and put it back together piece by piece. Nowadays a person, or rather a corporation, would *reproduce* a castle to look exactly like one in the old country. In some ways the reproduction would be better, neater. The wiring and plumbing would be hidden in the walls and the casement windows double glazed for draft prevention. But the stones would probably be ersatz, a clever blend of wire and cement. Winston thought about Europe and its castles and wondered if he'd ever get a chance to see them. The portcullis dropped noisily behind the van as it passed, closing off the courtyard. The sound was a little too final for Winston's comfort.

The *Hyorky* throbbed at the dock, ready to take Winston and Liam off to parts unknown. With the dark of the night meeting the dark of the river, the *Hyorky* looked like a ship hovering in a space port, its running lights eerie and otherworldly against the nothingness of the surrounding expanse. The illusion was shattered with a sweep of the van headlights. Dutch and Cynthia stood waiting at the dock, a somber welcoming committee; one grimly sentient, the other sensibly grim. Stepping from the vehicle, Winston watched and listened as Liam defrocked himself and Rolly hyperventilated beside him. Winston paid attention to the boat and the dock and the nearness of the water. How many times had he seen in the movies—the run, the jump, the submersion? The hollow, little reed breaking the surface, undetected by the confused pursuers. Where did they get those reeds?

"Come over here, please." Cynthia, who had been talking quietly to Conran over to the side, called to Dutch.

Much to Winston's disapproval, Liam had taken over the handling of the prisoner, his gun pressed hard into Winston's rib cage, a nagging reminder that escape might be impossible. Now Dutch had gone into the storage area and returned with some rope to bind his arms. Standing there allowing himself to be hog-tied, Winston couldn't be sure but the securing of the prisoner didn't seem particularly tight or binding, and Winston wondered if Dutch was providing him with a possible out once the adventure turned serious. Conran, who appeared to be the only one enjoying himself, accompanied Dutch onto the boat and up to the pilothouse. Conran's cheerful basso could be heard above the rumble of the *Hyorky's* engines. Winston was dismayed to hear the men discussing suitable sights for deep-sixing his weary body. Cynthia Shea actually gave him a little wave as she got into her car. Watching her drive away, Winston thought of Mary Bartlett and wondered if she had taken a swim without him. He would certainly welcome her lovely face at the moment, particularly if it was beaming at him from the shotgun side of a police car. Conran motioned for Liam to bring Winston aboard.

"Welcome aboard, Winston. A lovely night for a moonlight cruise."

"I'd just as soon be dancing," answered Winston.

"I admire your spunk, Winston, and you do know that I . . . the whole organization regrets this depressing turn of events . . . but . . ." Conran shrugged.

"I'm touched, Michael. I really am but don't you think someone is going to wonder what happened to the architectural historian who drove north to deliver a talk to a certain retreat. I have a date with Captain Sweetman in the morning . . ." Winston lied. ". . . don't you think he's going to inquire after my whereabouts?"

"All taken care of. Later tonight that lovely red automobile you drove north is going to fly off the road and plunge into the Hudson River from a very high point on route 6. It happens occasionally, I'm sorry to say. Usually they find the body but sometimes . . ."

Winston had to stop himself from arguing they couldn't do that because the car was rented.

"Where would you like to sit? In the salon or on the rear deck?"

"Doesn't a condemned man usually get the meal of his choice, not the seat?"

"I wish I could stay and exchange witty banter with you all night, Winston, but there's much to do. Take him in the salon, Rolly."

Winston could see Conran conferring with Liam and Dutch on the rear deck. For a man who had seen the world many times and experienced all things known to man, Dutch looked nervous and slightly confused. The man's shoulders had developed a rounded look and the eyes darted here and there,

247

alighting on the salon for a second and then flitting back to the face of Michael Conran. If Winston had a chance of freedom it would come with the intervention of Dutch, and possibly Rolly, on his behalf with Liam. At this point, Winston was more than agreeable to forgetting that he had ever seen or heard of Liam or the Oblates of Tranquil Deliverance. He would even return their retainer, with interest.

Conran stood on the dock and waved as the *Hyorky* pulled away, its engines coming to life with a cough and a roar. Winston indicated the liquor cabinet to Rolly.

"Mind if I have a drink? Scotch if you have it."

Rolly hesitated. "I guess so. I can't untie you though."

"Then just set it on the table before me. I could use a companion at the moment that I understand."

"Listen, pal, you have to believe I don't go along with this shit, no way. I'm having a lot of trouble with it, I mean that."

"You could do something about it."

Rolly shrugged. "I could, I know . . . but . . ." Shaking his head, Rolly disappeared out the door. It would be too much to think Rolly was actually going to talk with Liam so Winston looked around for something that might cut his bonds. The only thing available was a corkscrew. That wouldn't do it. Of course, he could save them some trouble and toss himself overboard. Winston thought of Justin Barefoot and how he looked when he floated up out of the rolling water: the needing eyes, the empty mouth, the elongated fingers. Fishfood. Not a happy ending.

And speaking of unhappy endings. Who killed Justin Barefoot? Winston thought he knew. You look from the peepholes to see if the dining hall is occupied and if not, you steal down and remove one of the weapons. You take the back exit from the castle and follow the tree line down to the boathouse. No one would ever see you. Unless . . . Winston wondered if Conran had bumped into Thomas Smelton moments before the old man had whacked Mr. Barefoot. Of course, Conran would have had no idea what Smelton was up to and he certainly wouldn't have brought it up later. None of the political do-gooders had anything to gain by killing Barefoot and bringing such focus onto the retreat. The thought of losing *The History* and the castle was too much for the "foolish fond old man." Winston became aware of the *Hyorky* coming to a stop. Liam and Rolly appeared at the door to the cabin.

"We need you outside, Mr. Wyc."

Liam sounded like his mother's cousins from Donegal.

"You wouldn't be from the North of Ireland, Liam?"

"Does not matter where *I* come from but to where you might be going, sir. Set out here, please."

Winston gave Rolly a concerned expression but the man only bent his head to look at the floor. Out on the rear deck, Winston checked to see how far the boat was from land but it was difficult to know in the extreme darkness. The wet wind that tossed his hair smelled of brine and fish.

"I think we should tie his legs," said Liam.

"It doesn't matter, I can't swim."

Liam gave Winston a sour smile and motioned for Rolly to find some hemp. Coming around the corner of the salon, Dutch dropped down onto the deck.

"You come to see me off?" asked Winston.

"You can't throw this man off my boat," said Dutch getting between Winston and Liam. The fire was back in his lantern eyes and the ropey veins stood high and tense on the sinewy arms. A little confused, Liam backed up two steps.

"Don't be a fool, man. You know this has nothing to do with you."

"I can't allow it. I'll take responsibility."

Rolly came up from below, a length of bailing wire in his hand. He looked from Dutch then to Liam. "What's up?"

"Your friend wants to let the man go. Talk some sense to him, will you?"

"What are you doing, Dutch?"

"We don't toss innocent people into the river, Rolly. We don't kill people."

"Yeah, but . . ." Rolly looked like he was about to cry.

"If you don't step aside, man, I'll have to shoot you." Liam's voice had gone quiet and low, and Winston watched as the gun came level with Dutch's stomach. "The other guy could take the boat over. Is that not right?" Liam spoke directly to Rolly.

"Well, I could . . . if I wanted."

Liam stepped away from the three men and over to the gunwale. He was a man who'd been in worse situations and it wouldn't take him long to sift through his alternatives and arrive at a plan of action. His existence depended on one of these men getting him to his destination and getting him there soon. Piloting the ship wasn't the problem. Liam had no idea where he was or in which direction to run.

"I'm going to count to five, Mr. Dace, and if you haven't gone back to the wheel I'm going to kill

250

you." Liam turned to Rolly. "And then I'm going to count to five again."

"Jesus," said Rolly under his breath.

"One, two . . ."

"Look, I hate to be such trouble, maybe . . ." Winston interrupted Liam's count.

"Shut up," snapped Liam. "Three . . ."

Dutch didn't have the look of a man about to leave. With shoulders squared and feet firmly placed, he appeared to elongate with each count, his head higher, his expression more determined.

Winston jumped up on one of the cushioned seats. "What? No plank?" Everyone stopped to look at him, their mouths slightly ajar. Leaping straight out, Winston hung in the air for a moment before falling for what seemed an eternity into the dark river, the surface solid, then giving way, taking him quickly down a chute of cold, black water. High above him two shots could be heard and then silence. Winston fought the impulse to panic. Realizing that his bonds were loosening, he had decided to take the plunge and hit the water. He certainly wasn't going to survive if Liam tied his legs together. The impact of the surface as he had entered the Hudson had pulled the rope up over his head and although still tied at the wrists, the rest of Winston's bindings floated limply above him in the darkness. Kicking dolphin style, Winston tried to put as much distance between himself and the *Hyorky* as he could before he needed to come up for air. Because of the night, he could not discern how far he was from breaking the surface, and so to avoid being spotted he stayed down longer than was healthy for him. Suddenly he felt faint, the pain in his chest overwhelming. He had to take a breath. Panic. Winston's legs failed to propel him any longer. Clawing at the water above him, he opened his mouth in a silent and watery scream. Barefoot's bloated face rose before him, the eyes wide, the mouth spread in a smile. The man's long fingers clutched at his calves. Winston wondered if you could tell if someone was crying under water. Then he blacked out.

Chapter 27

Sputtering, Winston came to life with Mary sitting on his chest, her mouth over his. Realizing that he was conscious, she smacked him hard across the face.

"What the . . . ? Give me a . . ." Winston winced as Mary raised her hand again.

"Shut up, you crazy bastard." Mary's face was white with fear. Tears ploughed two identical furrows down either side of her nose. "You can't scare people like this."

"Did I die and go to hell?"

"Thanks a lot, you prick."

Looking around him, Winston could see that he was on his back in the bottom of a small boat. It was still night and far off in the distance he could hear sirens, their keening sharp and strangely comforting. Rising, Mary scrambled to the stern of the boat and placing her hand on an idling outboard motor, brought it also to life. Winston had trouble kneeling as the skiff shot forward, planing out into the wind. Far off to the right, he could see the running lights of the *Hyorky*, a search beam making jerky circles of light on the water. A few deep breaths and Winston was able to join Mary at the stern.

"You're the most beautiful woman I've ever known." Winston kissed Mary's cheek.

"That's a little better."

"What happened?"

"It's a long story and I'll give you the details later, but basically I was in Dutch's apartment calling the police when I saw the *Hyorky* pull away from the dock." Mary had to raise her voice above the noise of the engine. "As soon as Conran got into his van, I took off down the shore to where my boat was stashed and followed you. I'd just caught up when I saw you jump over the side. What in the hell was that all about?"

"I'll explain later."

"I figured you'd pop up a little way from the boat, straight out, but you never did. All hell was breaking loose on the *Hyorky* so no one much noticed me. I wasn't supposed to be there." Mary took a moment to catch her breath and relaxed her voice. Winston turned to see if the *Hyorky* was still visible. Another boat with flashing red lights could be seen heading in the *Hyorky's* direction. Mary's face was turned slightly away, but Winston could see that she was crying again. Placing his hand on hers, he manipulated her fingers so that the engine reduced its speed and noise.

"Dutch tried to save me."

"He did?"

"If it hadn't been for him, I'd be dead right now."

"And not me?" Mary feigned being hurt.

"You know what I mean."

"I thought you were a goner. I'd almost given up and then I saw this rope floating on the surface of the water so I pulled it up and damned if you weren't there on the other end."

"Saved by the ties that bind. How poetic."

254

"Why don't you kiss me?" Mary always knew the right words—her reporter's training.

The two kissed and remained silent for the rest of the journey back to shore, Winston with his arm around Mary, Mary staring pensively into the middle distance. The boathouse was once again the scene of flashing blue lights and milling policemen.

"I think I know who killed Justin Barefoot," said Winston.

"Who?"

"Bozo the Senile."

"Smelton?"

"I'm sure of it. He so much as told me. It's a shame too, for I think the man was about to end his life of reclusiveness."

"Oh yeah. Look, let's talk about something else, okay?"

"What?"

"Vacations. You still checked into the Sherry-Netherland?"

Winston laughed. "I'd forgotten about that. I must owe them a fortune at this point. You have a good memory."

"The bane of the good reporter. Answer my question."

"I guess I am."

"Want company? And you better say yes or I turn this boat around and take you back where I found you."

"I'd love it if you joined me, Mary, the fisherman's beautiful daughter."

Mary smiled. "Good. Let's get you out of those wet clothes."

Mary lifted Winston's legs and sat on the chaise

with him. Reaching over, she picked up his glass and sniffed it.

"A little early for scotch, isn't it?"

"What? You running my life now? I'm preparing for the bill which will be waiting at the front desk when we check out in two hours."

"I never thought I'd enjoy vacationing on top of a sky scraper, but it's been real nice."

Nudging her with his toe, Winston smiled. "Where have you been?"

"I talked to Dutch."

Winston sat up. "You did?"

"One more item for the bill. I didn't think you'd mind."

"Uh huh. What's with Dutch? He's going to be okay?"

"He's going to be fine. Looks like he won't have to go to jail. With your story and his having taken a bullet, the authorities have decided to go easy on the old man. He said to say thank you."

"I should be thanking him. That's great news."

"You got that right, Winston love. Look, since we have two hours left on the room, why don't we put it to some use? I'm not going to see you again for a while. I have to head back north and take back my position as star reporter for the *New Holland Observer*." Mary ran her hand up Winston's leg, pulling the hair of his thigh.

"Ouch. You don't mean back to the boom-boom room."

"Boom, pal."

Winston laughed. "Boom."